Jackie Watson was born in Newcastle-upon-Tyne and lives with her partner and their adored Miniature Schnauzer in a former mining village, close to the banks of the Tyne. She is the author of the *Apokeri Bay* trilogy which was born out of a recurring dream. *Agnes Karapetsa is All at Sea* is the back story to one of the trilogy's characters and was inspired by deleted scenes from *Apokeri Bay.*

Praise for Jackie Watson

'As temperatures dropped at home, I found sunshine in this page-turner which transports readers to glorious Greece. ... This feel-good debut is perfect for all lovers of women's contemporary fiction, or anyone seeking sunshine.' *Living North Magazine* on *Apokeri Bay*

'I would defy anyone to resist visiting [Lefkada] after reading this gorgeous novel. Evocative, engaging and the perfect advert for this stunning setting, I enjoyed every word of this delightful story.' *Bookaholic Bex* on *Apokeri Bay*

'I read Apokeri Bay in one weekend! The gorgeous setting made me want to take a trip to Greece. A lovely, cosy romance read.' *Sally Grey* author of *Fertile Ground* on *Apokeri Bay*

'A Fantastic Holiday Read!!! ... The writer transported me to Greece from the first page with all the beautifully vivid descriptions, then when you add to this the vibrant characters and a story that does not go where you expect it to, each twist giving me an oh or ah moment along with some unknown Geordie facts!' *Goodreads review* on *Apokeri Bay*

'My favourite book so far this year ... It's all too easy to pick big authors whose work I know and trust or well publicised books. I was recommended this by a friend ... I am so pleased I bought this. It's definitely an 'unputdownable' book and reading it was very much time well spent. It's beautifully written with great characters & storyline and so much more than just a 'love story'. Thank goodness there's the second instalment on its way, I can't wait.' *Amazon review* on *Apokeri Bay*

'Brilliantly written and I couldn't put it down. Wow! I loved the first book, and I was so excited to be back in Apokeri with Anna and the family. I can honestly say that what I was expecting in the sequel was not what we got! But it was incredible!' *Amazon review* on *Saving Elora*

'Well-written, fast-paced and oozing tension, Jackie Watson quickly drew me into the fictional world she had created and I loved the sense of community that radiated from the pages … Tense, twisty, moving and engaging, Saving Elora is perfect for anyone who wants their escapist read with a side of danger.' *Emma's Biblio Treasures* on *Saving Elora*

'This novel had me hooked! Watson as usual does an amazing job of setting the scene and I felt once again transported to Greece and like I was right there alongside our main characters during this crazy ride. This author so effortlessly ties in the past and the present and keeps you hooked with interesting twists and turns, I enjoyed the whole mafia sub plot and the drama that ensues. I can't wait to see what Jackie comes up with next.' *Titleswtyler* on *Saving Elora*

'Wow! What a page turner. If you have read Apokeri Bay you must get Saving Elora now! If you haven't read Apokeri Bay... buy both!! You will not regret it. Awesome characters, amazing detail and superb storyline.' *Amazon review* on *Saving Elora*

'There are a lot more twists and turns within this storyline. I love how Jackie manages to make you think that you are on the Greek island along with Anna, by her descriptive writing …The book is filled with betrayal, crime, secrets, forgiveness and more, you won't be disappointed. It's a fast pace and enjoyable read, one to pop in your bag.' *Goodreads review* on *Saving Elora*

BY JACKIE WATSON

Apokeri Bay
Saving Elora
Agnes Karapetsa is All at Sea

AGNES KARAPETSA IS ALL AT SEA

ON ONE CRUISE, TWO LIVES ARE CHANGED FOREVER

Jackie Watson

First published in Great Britain in 2024 by Hawthorn Wren
This paperback edition published by Hawthorn Wren

A CIP catalogue record for this book is available from the British Library

ISBN: 978 1 7393404 3 8 (Paperback)
ISBN: 978 1 7393404 4 5 (Ebook)

For those who take a chance on dreams

Chapter One

The gleaming white cruise ship waited patiently alongside Valletta's quayside. In a few hours, three thousand tourists would embark on a fourteen-day luxurious Mediterranean getaway. But for now, calmness reigned.

Inside the five-star multi-storey floating hotel, crew members busied themselves with last-minute preparations. However, in the opulent Mariners cocktail lounge, ten members of an exclusive club relaxed. The natural banter belied the competitive nature as the tinkling of fake piano music played to non-existent guests.

Rodriguez, the flamboyant resident stand-up comedian tapped a swizzle stick against his Singapore Sling. 'I call to order the Floating Fantasy Football Club.' He cast a withering glance at Sebastian who was explaining to his hard-of-hearing mother back in Puebla how to increase the volume on her mobile. 'If you don't mind, I'd like to get started sometime today.'

The maître d' half-shouted to his mother that he'd call her back and returned an equally disdainful look. 'Keep your wig on, Roddy. You've plenty of time to strap on your corset and buff your nails before unleashing yourself on an unsuspecting audience.'

'Ladies, please,' Maria, the ship's senior photographer interjected in her sexy Marseille accent. 'Can we try the unthinkable and attempt to be civil to one another in our presence?'

'Hear, hear,' everyone chorused.

'As I was saying,' Rodriguez began but stopped as Maria nervously raised her hand.

'I've had somebody asking about the club.'

Silence descended and the air pressure dropped. This was a major breach of regulations. Nobody discussed the FFFC to any non-member without approval and even to one another the group regularly conversed in code. One could never be too careful who was listening.

Rodriguez's nostrils flared, an enraged warthog in a spandex shirt and kitten heels. 'Who is making enquiries?'

'Celeste,' Maria whispered, and all eyes focused on the resident bohemian artist sitting next to her.

Vlad flicked back his shoulder-length hair. 'Why are you all looking at me?'

'I believe you were on intimate terms with the pretty beautician, during our last cruise,' Sebastian pointed out.

'In other words, he was giving her one.' Tomas, the debonair first officer, smirked. He sat erect as if fearing to put a crease in his pristine, well-fitted white uniform. He never appeared in anything else and cut a dashing figure striding about the ship, basking in the admiring glances of passengers (and crew). Rodriguez often declared that the man probably went to bed in it. And the FFFC club members would smile, only because the Canadian's snide comments were borne out of jealousy for a long-lost pert bottom and washboard stomach.

'He was banging her brains out from what I heard,' Bettina - the willowy blonde dance teacher - added in disgust. It was no secret that Bettina and the young lady in question loathed one another. 'I mean really, Vlad, I thought you'd have had better taste. Heaven knows where she's been.'

'Well, what's a man to do, when the woman of his dreams continually refuses his advances?' Vlad suggestively raised an eyebrow at Bettina. 'Unless you've reconsidered?' The sexual tension crackled between the pair. 'You know we're perfect for one another. Both gorgeous, both artistic, both ... adventurous.'

Bettina crossed her long, shapely legs and fluttered mascara-coated eyelashes. 'In your dreams, Van Gough. But I understand as you're unable to have the best, you were forced to endure a cheap supermarket brand. All I'll say is whereas I'm discreet, Little Miss Blabbermouth can't keep her trap shut about anything for more than five minutes.'

'Excusez moi.' Maria rapped the table with flawlessly manicured nails. 'That's my friend you're talking about.'

'Come on,' Bettina replied and looked to everyone for confirmation. 'You know as well as I do that Celeste thrives on wheedling out the latest gossip from any unsuspecting victim and then broadcasting it. She's not called Radio Afloat for nothing.' There were collective nods and murmurings of agreement.

'Exactly,' Vlad interrupted, keen to maintain his innocence. 'She could have found out from anyone.'

'Did you leave your mobile unattended in her presence?' Rodriguez refused to be sidetracked as his voice dropped menacingly low.

'It-it's password protected.' Vlad fumbled in his leather trousers for his phone and held it up as evidence.

'I'm glad to see that,' Sebastian replied like a kindly professor. Agnes understood why the quietly spoken manager was so well respected by his team. He never raised his voice and was always a paragon of restraint (except when conversing with Rodriguez). 'But is it a strong password, son?'

Vlad fiddled with his gold bracelets. 'Erm—'

'For the love of God,' Rodriguez snapped and glared at each member. 'Please do not tell me that any of you have been stupid enough to use your date of birth or employee number.' Vlad quickly picked up his phone and frantically tapped away on the screen as Rodriguez leaned back in his seat and sighed. 'I weep for the future.'

Everyone exhaled slowly. Rodriguez's legendary temper remained under wraps. The volatile Canadian possessed a phenomenal work ethic and as the best compère and stand-up on the cruise ship circuit he was adored by guests and management. In a nutshell, he could blow his top at colleagues and get away with it.

'Shall we move on?' Maria clicked the mouse and as the league table popped up, they crowded around the screen. After six months, it was still all to play for. Rodriguez was naturally in the lead; the man was unbeaten in two decades. He was a ruthless competitor with a relaxed attitude towards morals.

Even after three years, Agnes trod warily around the acid-tongued diva. She knew never to confuse his Vancouver accent with a Californian one, as it was a sure-fire way to set him off. So Sebastian took great pleasure in spinning a yarn to new staff that Rodriguez was LA born and bred and his dreams of lifting a heavyweight boxing title had sadly been dashed due to an addiction to Dunkin' Donuts. In his heyday, he was the Mighty Bull Shark but his fall from grace earned him the nickname Podgy Porpoise. Sebastian would confide to each wide-eyed newcomer that it was a great secret, never to be uttered. Agnes had heeded the warning, but others didn't. Those who blabbed to Rodriguez when he was in a good mood suffered nothing more than a recital of the facts through gritted teeth. Those unfortunate souls who cornered him in a bad mood had strips torn off them. And as they'd been told to keep quiet, the terrified crew members had to stand and take everything thrown at them.

At twenty-three, Agnes was the youngest and the only non-public-facing member of the club. She'd only ever had one run-in with Rodriguez after foolishly complaining that as a junior chef, slaving away in the kitchen for all hours, she was at a serious disadvantage in striking up conversations with passengers. She'd endured a ten-minute tongue-lashing and had never raised the topic again.

'This is the final fortnight of our friendly competition,' Rodriguez announced. Vlad snorted but was quickly hushed. 'So, the lower positions are all to play for. Me winning is a foregone conclusion.'

'Hey!' Tomas butted in. 'I should be in second place, not third bottom.' There was a collective intake of breath and Agnes braced herself for the inevitable.

'How dare you call into question the decision to dock you points?' Rodriguez exploded and hurled his swizzle stick at the Italian's head. The younger man easily ducked, and the glass javelin harmlessly bounced across the carpet. 'You're lucky not to be disqualified after an outrageous attempt at match-fixing. Rule six clearly states no manager can have prior dealings with their choice of player.'

Tomas began to protest but Sebastian held up his hand. 'Don't try to deny it, lad. We've all heard the evidence from the player in question. She let it slip to Roddy over a late-night drinking session and he happened to be recording the whole conversation. Once I was presented with the evidence, there was nothing I could do.'

'Were you worried I was going to finally knock you off your perch?' Tomas rounded on Rodriguez. 'That you had to stoop to dubious tactics. You just can't bear to lose, can you?'

'Don't blame someone else for your cheating,' Agnes interjected. She rarely spoke up at the meetings and again questioned how she'd been permitted entry into this highly restricted club.

Each member was gorgeous, witty, and immensely talented. They all possessed a natural confidence and charisma that erected an invisible wall around them and at the same time acted as an irresistible lure. People bent over backwards for them, craved their approval and their adoration (often resulting in bitchiness if they didn't get it). Each one could have stepped into a Hollywood blockbuster, or a slick US hit show where nobody fumbled over their words or had a hair out of place. They were loved and (for some) hated in equal measure.

'Oh, the malevolent vulture finds her voice,' Tomas teased with an exaggerated scowl and hunched shoulders.

She laughed along with everybody else but straightened in her seat. As a tall child, she'd developed a habit of stooping which she often fell back into. Her hooked nose and a naturally stern expression didn't help matters. It wasn't the first time she'd been likened to an unattractive scavenging bird with her wiry frame and long limbs. But she could give as good as she got and there was no malice intended. The atmosphere around the table lightened and she was reminded as to why she remained part of the group. The seven of them bounced off one another, and it gave them all a safe place to let off steam – even if the jokes were usually at the expense of those they were paid to look after.

The Floating Fantasy Football Club (FFFC for short) had run for years, and Agnes supposed there was a similar setup on many cruise ships. For all the wonderful places they visited, crew members quickly became bored and needed a distraction from visiting the same ports over and over again, working all hours and often dealing with the excessive demands of management and paying guests. Although she didn't agree with his tactics, Agnes understood why Tomas had broken the rules to claim the top spot. Dethroning Rodriguez was everyone's ambition. The man was an insufferable winner and Agnes was willing to bet if anyone else had uncovered Tomas's deceit they'd have kept quiet. As things now stood it was going to take a miracle for anyone to get within sniffing distance of him.

Sebastian was reiterating the rules (just in case anyone else felt like cheating) and then quickly summarised the league table. He touched the bottom row with a long knickerbocker glory spoon and grinned. On each cruise, Sebastian started with high hopes which were always dashed and (much to everyone's relief) he'd always end up dead last. Nobody wanted that position, and it wasn't only because of pride. Receiving the wooden spoon came with the unenviable task of posting the running totals for the next season. With a myriad of ways to score points, it was a nightmare job and Agnes suspected only Sebastian and Rodriguez understood them all.

'In fourth place, we have our youngest and newest member, Agnes.' Sebastian nodded in her direction with a fatherly smile. 'In her second season, she's showing strong promise and is one to watch out for.'

There was a murmur of agreement and Agnes flushed with pride. She'd been abysmal in her first season due to a combination of cautiousness and an inability to grasp the scoring mechanism. Nothing was written down, so she constantly sought clarification from an ever-patient Maria. Three years ago, Agnes had arrived as an eager twenty-year-old, excited, and ambitious to become an excellent chef. She was from northern Greece and lived miles away from the coast, so loved life at sea. As a keen amateur artist, all her free time was spent drawing, sketching or painting – the results of which she sent home to her family, friends and long-term boyfriend. However, the long-distance relationship had floundered and after only a few months she was single and heartbroken. It had seen her eagerly volunteer to cover people's shifts. She never took time off and became increasingly withdrawn. After several weeks, Maria put her petite foot down and refused to tolerate a miserable room-mate. She dragged Agnes off the ship to go horse riding, instructed her to draw something every morning and (for some reason) brought her along to an FFFC meeting. Initially, Agnes refused to join. It wasn't her type of thing and besides she'd be no good and everyone would laugh at her. But Maria had kept chipping away at the Greek granite resolve until finally Agnes had cracked and agreed to give it a go. Thank goodness for Sebastian that first season, otherwise she would have been last. But gaining in confidence she was slowly making improvements.

Sebastian cleared his throat. 'In second place is Maria with a consistent performance this season, and out in front is Rodriguez. No surprise there.'

'Jealous, per chance?' Rodriguez lounged back in his seat and grinned like the cat with the proverbial cream. 'I don't know why we don't call the result now. I mean, nobody can catch me.'

'It isn't over till the fat lady sings.' Sebastian haughtily stared at his opponent squeezed into a tub chair. 'Or should that be until the podgy entertainer holds out for another encore.' Maria sniggered, as did a few others around the table. Rodriguez loved to milk the audience for applause. But there was no denying the man was brilliant with lightning-fast comebacks. Sebastian coughed and it was enough to restore order. 'In a couple of hours, we'll welcome our—'

'Victims,' Vlad interrupted.

'Targets,' Bettina prompted.

'Deluded fools,' Tomas supplied.

'Play-things,' Rodriguez added in a tone that sent an unpleasant shiver up Agnes's spine.

'Guests. We will welcome our guests aboard,' Sebastian managed through pursed lips. 'Remember, you have until ten o'clock tonight before the window opens and it will then close at midnight tomorrow. As soon as I receive your candidates you can start accumulating points. Whether you decide to submit early or late is entirely up to you. Both have their advantages and disadvantages. Tomorrow is a day at sea, and I encourage you to use the time wisely.'

The FFFC was not your standard fantasy football league. As Tomas was fond of saying, they played with a different set of balls. The name was a front for a more dubious game. Agnes nicknamed the group the United Nations of Deceit. Seven members and seven nationalities. Maria preferred FFM – Free From Morals. Harsh but true.

At the start of each cruise, team members picked a passenger(s) and once they were locked in, the seduction began. It was up to each member as to how they approached their targets, but the name of the game was to rack up as many points as possible with each kiss, cuddle, canoodle, roll in the sack and so on. There were any number of ways to score but weirdly (Agnes thought) for a game of deceit, it was based on trust. Members submitted their points each evening which were then shared with the group the following morning. Team members could score extra points depending on the status of their target. A singleton gained no extra points but if the person was in a relationship, then there was a sliding scale. The greatest points were awarded if a target was in a long-term relationship with their partner on board. There were also extra points if the target bought the team member gifts; if they fell in love with the team member; if the target broke up with their partner; and the jackpot (which nobody had ever hit) was if the target proposed. There was also the opportunity to play a joker for twenty-four hours, whereby all points were doubled. It was this tactic that Rodriguez excelled at. In Agnes's first season, the man had broken up six long-term relationships.

Team members adopted different strategies. Rodriguez, Tomas, and Maria went all out to win. The men tended to focus on one individual per cruise, whereas Maria played the numbers game. All three submitted their selection at the earliest opportunity. Agnes on the other hand had taken part for fun, to maybe find someone nice to chat to and even steal a kiss. She missed being in a couple and refused to 'screw the crew' which was part and parcel of life afloat it seemed. Agnes selected someone who appeared single and always backed off if they were attached. Well, that was how it had started. But as the months ticked by, her strong moral code flexed. If the target wasn't single but was happy to play away on holiday, who was she to object or feel guilty? And this was how she was slowly climbing the league table. Was it so wrong to eagerly open the FFFC message each morning and grin at leapfrogging over those who'd played the game for years? For ambitious Agnes it wasn't about taking part, it was about winning.

Maria checked her watch and shut the laptop. 'Time to make tracks. I need to take up my prime position to welcome our prey on board.'

Chapter Two

There was always a buzz of excitement when the new arrivals boarded. Even the most battle-weary crew member still had that kernel of anticipation. Like the start of a new year, who knew what the next batch of passengers might bring? Agnes had wangled an hour out of the kitchen and, with Rodriguez and Sebastian, she hung over the guardrail on the top deck and scanned the eager tourists. The early morning air was filled with all the expected sounds and sights as thousands of people were funnelled aboard and the slick operation would take a few hours. In the sunshine, the impressive walled city of Valletta glowed. Agnes loved Europe's smallest capital city and given the chance, she would love to spend half a day wandering along its limestone streets to sketch the colourfully painted balconies and the baroque architecture. But for now, she was keeping an eye out for her star player.

Down below, Maria easily steered the guests into position with a smile and small talk. Photographing the guests by the gangway was a huge money spinner for the cruise liner, and for the chatty French woman it provided a perfect opportunity to narrow down her selection of targets.

'That girl's a pro,' Rodriguez remarked in a rare display of admiration.

Maria subtly homed in on the male groups of passengers and the trio watched as she flirtatiously arranged them with a casual arm on the shoulder or a hand on the waist and words of encouragement. And as a result, Maria's photographs were always snapped up. She excelled at capturing the atmospheric architecture along with relaxed and happy holidaymakers. There were occasional grumblings by the other photographers at Maria's tactics, but as their pictures never sold as well, management dismissed any complaints and if anyone chose to take it further, they'd find their contract wasn't renewed.

From their elevated position, it was impossible to hear the conversations, but Agnes knew her room-mate would be gabbling away in her seductive accent, quickly establishing a rapport with the men passing her way. The elfin brunette had a distinct advantage over many FFFC competitors. Armed with a camera, she could easily walk up to anyone and engage in conversation.

Even in late September, the heat was starting to build, and Agnes was giving thought to moving when raucous laughter rose above everything else. A group of seven men were on the gangway and Agnes was willing to bet they'd had a skinful. They all appeared to be egging on one man. He was hanging back, as if unwilling to take part. From her position, she could only make out his average height, average build and dark skin. Suddenly, he lunged and slapped Maria's arse to roars of laughter. Maria simply did what she always did to every other group and after she took their photos, they moved off.

'Him,' Agnes spat. 'That male chauvinist asshole. I'll make him pay for that.'

Rodriguez raised a perfectly plucked eyebrow. 'Hardly a gentleman, is he? Lord, I hope he's not Canadian. Bringing the name of my homeland into disrepute.'

'Or Mexican,' Sebastian added. 'Are you sure, Agnes? You don't know anything about the man. Do you not want to find out about him first?'

'She's made her decision,' Rodriguez snapped. 'Sexist Pig is locked in.'

Sebastian pushed up his wire-framed glasses. 'I think you'll find rule sixteen states that the official selection must be non-verbal. Agnes is well within her rights to change players.' Rodriguez puffed up like a bullfrog, but Sebastian gave an evil grin. 'Be careful, Roddy. I think I just heard your girdle twang.

Remember, I've played the game far longer than you, and I stick to the rules.'

'Fine, have it your way.' And without a backwards glance, the usually witty man stropped off as Sebastian hummed the *Rocky* anthem.

'What is it between you two?' Agnes sighed. 'All you do is snipe at each other.'

Sebastian gave a sad smile. 'It's a long story. Let me know if you change your mind.' And then he was gone.

Chapter Three

Agnes pushed the staff-only door open and trudged down the well-worn carpet. It was late and after a full day of cooking, the cloying scent of kitchen fat, garlic and spices clung to her clothes, skin and hair like a leech.

Even now, people bustled up and down the corridor. With over a thousand employees, there were always comings and goings. Agnes turned the key but surprisingly the compact, twin-bunked room was open. She'd expected resident party-girl Maria to be out and about, assessing her targets and clocking up the points. With artwork and family snapshots, their space was as welcoming as you could make a basic, utilitarian cell. Everything was stripped back to the bare minimum. A functional space and nothing more. It was undoubtedly designed that way. Management ensured a prominent shift rota was affixed in every cabin, which was laughable. They could have saved themselves the time and effort and just tacked a big piece of paper with SLOG YOUR GUTS OUT emblazoned across it. What the timetable said and what you did were two very different things. Most of the crew got up, went to work, squeezed in an hour or so of downtime and then went to bed. However, the reason for Maria being at home was probably to do with what was shoehorned onto their collapsible shared shelf. Management called it a table, which was a joke. It certainly wouldn't fit place settings for two.

'That's fast work, even for you,' Agnes commented as she stripped off her uniform. The cabin was far too small for modesty. 'I reckon you've got a shot at winning this season. The first full day and you've already gained points. What did you have to do for those? Or don't I want to know?'

Maria stretched out, catlike, and yawned. 'You know I'd tell you all the sordid details. However, my luck is out. The person who sent that gorgeous bouquet has already been claimed – by you.'

'What?' Agnes blurted out, causing her dirty clothes to sail past the open laundry basket. 'Sexist git sent those?' Maria nodded and handed over a pretty card with neat handwriting.

Please accept this bouquet and chocolates as a heartfelt apology for my appalling conduct yesterday morning. It's absolutely no excuse but I did it for a bet. I've got a list of them to complete during my stag cruise.

Kind regards

Tony Acebi

Agnes plonked herself on the other fold-down chair. 'Oh no, he can't be getting married.'

Maria passed across a luxury box of opened truffles. 'Help yourself. I can't stop eating them, even though I feel sick. You're going to have to relax those morals, my girl, if you want to stay in the game. Or pick a new target.'

Agnes checked the time. It was 00:07. 'Crap, I'm too late. It's gone midnight. And besides I wouldn't know who else to choose. While you've been swanning about on board all day, I've been stuck in a windowless oven.'

'Get in that shower, woman. You're stinking our cubicle out with fried onions and garlic,' Maria retorted and despite her earlier comment chomped down on another truffle. 'You know as well as I do that a day at sea is the toughest gig. I've been on my feet all day, snapping the punters and constantly appearing ever so chirpy. I'm exhausted.'

Agnes rubbed her greasy face. 'Sorry, I'm just annoyed at being too eager with my choice. Who did you end up picking?'

Her room-mate grinned. 'Not Tony's gang, that's for sure. I'm not joking, everywhere I went on the ship I could hear at least one of them. I think their volume is stuck on annoyingly loud. Anyway, I've gone for a sensitive Irish chap on holiday with his mother. I'm hoping he doesn't turn out to be gay. Then there's a stag do from Berlin.'

Agnes choked on a truffle. 'You're going after the whole group? That's a tad ambitious.'

'Don't be stupid, I'm not a total slut.' Maria dramatically rolled her eyes. 'Only two of them. But not the stag. That's a step too far, even for me. And then—'

'What, there's more!'

'Just the one,' Maria declared and firmly closed the box of hand-crafted chocolates. 'He's also French and ex-military. So super-fit. I keep telling you, girl. You need backups.'

'Are you planning on sleeping during this trip?' Agnes called over her shoulder and ducked inside the ensuite as a pillow hit the closed door.

She stripped off her underwear and let the lukewarm water wash her clean. If only for a few hours. Her elbow banged against the wall, and she cursed. The room was so tiny it was possible to sit on the toilet and have a shower at the same time, which came in handy sometimes. She forcefully shut off the shower and swore as the towel dropped onto the wet floor. Her position in this season's league table was going to be diabolical. Like Maria, there was no way she was going to seduce a groom-to-be. Her competition was over before it had even begun.

Chapter Four

Strictly speaking, galley staff worked a maximum of twelve hours straight. But what happened on board, stayed on board. All that management cared about was that the food was excellent, and the guests were happy. Okay, that wasn't entirely true. The à-la-carte option had to be amazing. For the general masses, as long as the standard hit good enough for nobody to complain that was fine. On the plus side, it meant Agnes had an agreement with colleagues to allow her time off to indulge in her childhood horse-riding passion. As the best photographer on board, Maria had first pick of which excursions she photographed (her demands for a helper were naturally approved) and it saw Agnes tag along as the baggage handler.

Clattering down the gangplank, her mobile beeped and the latest league table results popped through. Things were not going well for the FFFC members. Despite extensive research, Rodriguez was incensed to discover that his target was well and truly straight. He stormed about the place in platform heels, outraged that a passenger so obviously gay was refusing to accept his true calling. The fact the Mancunian optician appeared happily married with two children did nothing to convince the comedian otherwise. Tomas had been caught in a passionate embrace with his twenty-year-old target. Her Bulgarian weightlifting father (whose neck was wider than Agnes's waist) had threatened to rip off the first officer's testicles if he came anywhere near his only child or any other female on board. With no chance of winning, Tomas had wisely decided to withdraw from the competition and protect his manhood.

Surprisingly, Maria was making no headway with any of her choices. The sensitive Irish chap was gay, the ex-military man turned out to be someone Maria went to school with, and the stag do party were too busy in one-upmanship to notice her. And to everyone's equal horror and delight, Sebastian withdrew himself entirely from the FFFC. And the reason? He was smitten. The maître d' refused to disclose their identity and would only state it had always been his intention to quit when he found his true love. He glided around in a bubble of happiness and managed to be even more charming, polite and wonderful to everyone. And despite their best and most devious efforts, nobody could work out who it was. Those remaining in the game had scored a few points here and there but much to Rodriguez's relief he was still way out in the lead. Agnes believed this was the reason why he'd shown a rare display of generosity and agreed to act as temporary score master. There was now an undercurrent of desperation amongst the rest of the group. Nobody wanted to be last and get lumbered with the nightmare job of scoring the following season.

The early morning sun was cloaked in a thin layer of cloud which dropped the temperature enough for Agnes to be glad of her jumper and jacket. Maria rifled through her rucksack, double-checking everything. It was a pointless exercise as Agnes was carrying duplicates of everything.

'I don't know why you're bothering to check, we cross-referenced everything before breakfast. Why don't—'

A burst of laughter made the pair look up.

'Oh no.' Maria plastered a dazzling smile on her elfin face and waved to Tony's stag do. 'They're the biggest bunch of dickheads going. Especially the best man leading out the troops.'

Swaggering ahead with shades and stubble was an ebony-skinned barrel of a bloke. Smoothing down his wrinkle-free shirt and chinos, his irritatingly loud voice carried across the quayside. As he bragged about screwing some poor unfortunate in every conceivable position, Agnes was strongly reminded of a wide-mouthed toad. She gulped down water to wash away the taste of bile.

'Hey guys,' he yelled at catching sight of the two women. 'Looks like we've got two fine fillies joining us this morning. I wouldn't mind getting in the saddle with one of them.' Braying with laughter, he slapped the back of an older bloke and all the younger men sniggered along with him.

Agnes tilted her head away. 'I feel sick.'

'Hey, Jahmar,' Tony Acebi yelled from the rear. 'You'll give us cockneys a bad name.'

'Too late,' Maria whispered.

***

The thirty-minute bus journey was tolerable, but only because Agnes grabbed the front seat with the excuse that she needed to practice her abysmal French with their Corsican driver. As usual, he laughed and started chatting to her in English. Unfortunately for Maria, she'd been sequestered to take group shots and capture the stag in his latest get-up of a giant sombrero, hairy poncho, gun belt, lasso, and spurs. The man looked ridiculous. How Maria chatted away merrily was beyond Agnes. However, the bus had barely ground to a halt before the Frenchwoman jumped out.

The stables sat at the bottom of a steep-sided valley and were owned by Cynthia, a sinewy woman in worn denim who immediately stamped her mark. 'Stand in your ability groups.' She motioned to three markers in the dust. 'Advanced, intermediate and beginner.' After cross-referencing everyone with the pre-filled forms, she waved them forward. 'Time to pair you up.'

It took longer than expected to get sorted as Jahmar dug his heels in about Tony wearing the stupid sombrero. Agnes silently fumed at the delay but at least by then the sun had burned off the clouds. It was eventually agreed that the enormous bright red contraption could be plonked over the riding hat. However, the wait allowed Agnes to notice that the more Tony's friends boasted about the stag's stellar horse-riding abilities, the quieter he became. He was a reverse jack-in-the-box, folded in on himself, and uneasiness built in Agnes, atop a sedate grey mare.

'I'm sorry,' Cynthia mouthed, mistaking Agnes's concern for annoyance. 'I've had to pair you with the old man as we're a horse down today.'

Agnes leaned forward in her saddle, keeping her voice low. 'I don't think our man on the black stallion has a clue about horses.'

Cynthia's eyes widened in disbelief. 'They've all stated their abilities and signed their disclaimers. Are you sure?'

Agnes glanced over to Tony and while the others laughed and joked at Jahmar, not a trace of a smile crept over his drawn face. 'His mates keep giving him stupid bets because it's his stag do and I think this might be one of them.'

'One last check,' Cynthia called out. 'Is everyone happy with their choice of horse?' A chorus of yes. 'Does anyone want to swap?' A chorus of no.

'Come on,' Jahmar barked. 'We've paid good money for this trip. Everyone's fine. Stop wasting time.'

Cynthia and Agnes locked eyes. There was nothing they could do, other than brand the paying guests liars. The older woman moved to the head of the line. 'Let's go.'

The trail set off along the valley that climbed up to a boulder-strewn landscape, far above the Mediterranean. The group would stop at the highest point for photos, coffee, and cake at a shepherd's hut before looping back down. Setting off at a leisurely pace amongst the dappled shade of the trees, they tracked along the side of a shallow stream. The sun sparkled on the clear water as it meandered slowly over the pebbles. A school of fish darted into the shadows with a flash of silver. Agnes loved horse riding, the chance to immerse herself in nature. She was a passionate chef, driven to succeed, but still needed to escape the confines of the kitchen and reset. It also reminded her of happy times with her father.

Before he—

No, she abruptly terminated those thoughts. She still couldn't shake the anger, even after all these years. Like the water the horses were now crossing, her rage could be stirred up at any time and was the main reason for leaving home. How could she remain with so many painful memories? She inhaled deeply. The scent of wild herbs and baked earth acted as a stress-busting tonic, and she tilted her head up to the warming sun. It was going to be a beautiful day.

She was last in line, partly because her horse was the slowest but also for maximum peace and quiet. Although he was on the fastest steed, Tony was directly ahead, and luckily Toad Man was far enough away for his irritating nasal laughter to be masked by the stream.

They trotted between sunshine and shade and Tony dropped further and further back. As the track widened, she drew alongside. His wide eyes stared ahead, his knuckles gripped the reins, and he was praying. The tension radiated off him and a light breeze would probably snap him in two. She dropped back in behind until they halted a few minutes later.

'Well done, everyone,' Cynthia called out. 'We're going to stop for a break and give Maria time to capture some photos. Feel free to dismount if you wish.'

Tony slid to the ground and wobbled across to a boulder. As he collapsed, Agnes jumped to the ground and approached him. It was time to be the bigger person.

'Hi there, I'm sorry to interrupt. It's Tony, isn't it?' She stuck out her hand and received a clammy one in return. 'I was hoping you could help me?'

He nodded tentatively. 'I can try.'

'It's rather embarrassing actually.' She fidgeted with her jacket zip. 'The thing is, I've chosen the wrong horse. Henri is too much for me but I-I don't want to admit my fears to the whole group. I was wondering, or – let's be honest – I'm begging you to swap with me.'

'Are … are you sure?' His hazel brown eyes flicked over to where the grey mare was nonchalantly munching a patch of long grass, while the stallion snorted and stamped the ground. 'I'd hate to spoil your fun.'

Agnes sat beside him and whispered (although the others were too far away to hear). 'Believe me, I'd be so relieved if you would.'

'Of course, I'd be happy to help.'

He had a nice smile; it improved his rather plain and pockmarked features.

'Thank you so much. You're a lifesaver.' She blew out a sigh of relief and sprung up. 'I'll go and let Cynthia know.'

While Maria snapped photos of a happy Tony lassoing his mates, Agnes quickly explained everything to the stable owner.

'You're an angel.' Cynthia embraced her tightly. 'I can relax now that I know de Gaulle is in your capable hands.'

It was then time to saddle up and, for the next hour, Agnes was lost in the beauty of Corsica.

Chapter Five

As Cynthia saw to the horses, Maria scuttled back and forth, capturing the group antics and the fantastic plateau views. As Agnes was never needed, she snuck off with a milky coffee and a slice of fiadone. She parked herself on a favourite rock and sank her teeth into the sumptuous Corsican cheesecake. This was the life. The rocky landscape dropped away a short distance from the shepherd's hut, in the distance the sea shimmered, and overhead a buzzard lazily circled.

'I think our feathered friend has got the right idea.' A husky male Caribbean voice made her jump. It belonged to a well-built and weather-beaten man. Due to his age, Agnes wondered if he was Tony's father. 'It's getting a bit noisy over there for me. Do you mind if I join you?'

'Of course not.' She brushed the rock free of its fine layer of dust, and he sat. 'I saw Tony and his friends board the ship but I don't remember seeing you.'

He shook his head and glanced over to the men who appeared to be re-enacting a gun fight from an old western. 'Unfortunately, I was unable to get a seat on the same flight as them and boarded a few hours later.' Agnes was sure she heard relief in his voice and suppressed a smirk. She nodded when he asked if she worked on the ship. 'It must be hard work, dealing with the likes of that rabble.'

Agnes smiled. 'Well, I'm in the kitchen so I escape the worst of it.'

He sipped his coffee and shifted to get a better position. 'That was a very commendable thing you did back there, young lady.' She remained silent, unsure how to respond. 'Saving Tony from that brute of a stallion.'

'Please, call me Agnes.' She stuck out her hand. His palm was rough. A working man's handshake. Firm, no-nonsense.

'Pleased to meet you. I'm Patrick.' He glanced over to where Jahmar was receiving congratulatory backslaps after boasting about bedding the Latvian dance teacher. Agnes laughed inwardly. So that's how Bettina had suddenly jumped up the league table this morning. Well, it couldn't happen to a nicer bloke. Patrick grimaced. 'I'm sorry about him. Unfortunately, there's always one in every group.'

'How do you know Tony?' She was trying to trace a likeness in the creased face of Patrick and the boyish looks of Tony. But she couldn't see it. Maybe her guess had been wrong.

'I've known him since he was a snotty-nosed kid. His daddy, God rest his soul, and Tony sat next to me at the match. But for the last decade, it's been just the youngster and me.'

'He must mean a lot to you.' She knew nothing about football fans. Did they usually socialise with one another outside the stadium? 'A two-week cruise isn't cheap. Especially our company's.'

Patrick smiled indulgently. 'He's worth his weight in gold that one. Looks after his momma and three older sisters. That's not easy; he's sacrificed a lot and I'm proud of him. He had big shoes to fill.'

It was an insight Agnes hadn't expected. But then again, hadn't Tony apologised to Maria with flowers and chocolates?

'Hey, old man,' Tony yelled across the grass, casting aside his sombrero. 'Enough flirting. I want a photo of us two and this amazing view.'

A mouthful of fiadone caught in her throat.

Chapter Six

Agnes lay in the pitch black. From below, Maria's gentle breathing floated upwards with the ever-present drone of the ship's engines.

Nothing out of the ordinary had awoken her, except the routine of an early start. What was the time? She smiled at her phone display – 05:10. It only ever varied by five minutes either way. She carefully swung her tanned legs into space and her outstretched toes felt for the bottom bunk. She dropped to the floor and flicked on a side light before quietly donning warm clothes and grabbing her backpack.

'Please don't tell me it's time to get up,' a sleepy voice mumbled.

'It's just after five.' There was a string of French expletives. 'Serves you right for staying out late.' Agnes sniggered and clicked the cabin door shut.

Usually, the corridor thronged with staff hurrying backwards and forwards while dodging delivery trolleys. But for now, it was eerily quiet. Her cabin was windowless, like the kitchen, and she emerged mole-like on the top deck, shivering in the pre-dawn air. Another day, another port. This time it was Livorno, Italy. She unfolded her music stand and clipped the battered sketch pad in place. It was time to finish her drawing and with enough light from inside she set to work capturing the remaining houses as the sun slowly emerged above the horizon. The stupidly early sketching was now a habit. At first, it was done with grumbling and mutterings, something else to take up her precious minutes, but now Agnes couldn't do without it. She was highly disciplined (having read all top chefs were) so trained herself to rise at the same time every morning and grab an hour before work. She loved the energy and the creative arena of a professional kitchen. There was no better place to be; it was her calling. But she also needed this quiet me time before most of the ship came to life. A passenger ran past, and they nodded to one another but soon she was oblivious to the woman lapping the upper deck.

'Are you drawing another dimension?'

Her short sharp yell echoed across the water and three seabirds shot off the guardrail, arched overhead and then landed fifty metres away, angrily ruffling their feathers.

'I'm so sorry.' Tony's badly bitten fingernails hovered over a thick pencil gash. 'I've totally ruined your wonderful drawing.'

She deftly erased the black line. 'It's all gone. Nothing to worry about.'

His frown deepened. 'No, you can still see the awful groove. I've made a right mess of it. As usual.'

'So, are you off to Pisa today?' she prompted to distract him. It tended to be the pilgrimage of choice for all the guests, but she was surprised when he shook his head.

'Oh, no. All the lads and me are major movie buffs and obsessed with James Bond, so we're off to Siena.' Agnes's face drew a total blank. 'Jahmar heard a rumour that they're going to film scenes for the next movie there. So we thought, let's go and check it out. Get ahead of the game.'

She shook her head. How bizarre. She knew places made a fortune offering film location excursions. Their cruise ship did it. But she'd never heard of visiting somewhere because it might appear in a film. 'Movies aren't my thing.'

With arms outstretched, he dramatically threw himself backwards against the ship and slid slowly onto a bench, clutching his heart. The pantomime performance made her laugh, but he still looked utterly appalled. 'Please tell me you've heard of James Bond.'

She laughed again and nodded. 'My stepmother had quite a thing for Pierce Brosnan. In fact, she still does.'

'My mum's the same.' He grinned and dug his hands further into his pockets. 'So, if films aren't your passion, what is?'

'Cooking is number one. Horse riding two and then it'd be this.' She smoothed the paper down on the stand. He tentatively ran his finger over the groove and his hazel eyes reflected sadness. His melancholy struck a chord, and she dug around in her bag.

'Here, take a look at this.' She handed him a dog-eared A4 notepad. 'This should hopefully make you feel better.'

He flicked through the rippled pages. 'Wow, you're prolific – landscapes, still life, portraits. But what happened?'

'My room-mate accidentally knocked a glass of lager over the whole thing. So it means I won't lose sleep over a barely visible pencil mark.'

'You must've been gutted,' he said wistfully and stared at her favourite drawing taken from a photograph. She was ten and sitting proudly on a pony with her papa holding the reins. 'I always wanted to be an artist,' he continued. 'But someone told me I was wasting my time and I needed to earn a decent living. It wasn't a proper job or one that made any money. So, I became a mind-numbingly boring IT specialist instead.'

Agnes bristled. She wasn't particularly fussed about Tony but hated when people thought they had the right to stomp on others' dreams. Had it been his mate, Jahmar? She rummaged around in her backpack again.

'There you go. Think of it as an early wedding present.'

He hesitantly took the spiral-bound notepad and three pencils as if he was waiting for her to snatch them back. 'Are you sure?'

'Why don't you draw something for your bride-to-be? As a surprise. I'm sure she'd love it.' It was a shy smile, and she imagined him as a kid sitting next to Patrick at a football match. 'Papa died when I was fourteen.' The words were out before she could stop them. Why had she told him that? She never mentioned her father to anyone.

He leaned against the guardrail and clutched his notepad like a cherished Christmas present. 'How did it happen?'

'He took a bend too fast on a moped. No helmet. Game over.' Her voice was deadpan, but even after a decade she was still furious at him. How dare he leave her, cutting her carefree teenage years short? Instantly she'd become the emotional support for her stepmother and a surrogate parent to three half-brothers. And the way he died, so incredibly stupid, so preventable. And the worst bit? He shouldn't have even been there. Why hadn't he waited for the taxi? Instead of roaring off into the darkness, half-drunk.

'I'm really sorry.' Tony's hand slid easily along the rail to squeeze hers. And to her immense surprise, she grasped it tightly. She wasn't a demonstrative person, and even less so after her father's funeral. She rarely cried now and clamped down on any emotion that reflected weakness. Her natural haughty expression usually held people back (except Maria), so it was strange for someone she barely knew to reach out to her. It was nice. He gave one final squeeze before letting go. 'He'd be so proud of you.'

She nodded mutely and glanced over to Livorno's impressive old Renaissance fortress. The Italian city was a major economic hub, and with its massive seaport it was already gearing up for a new day. Not that many of the passengers would see it. They'd stream off the boat and into a line of coaches and taxis to be ferried to better-known places. Only those frequently returning guests thought to explore the city's urban waterways, central market, museums and beaches. And with all you could possibly eat on board, very few sampled the city's amazing seafood. All those Livorno experiences would be bypassed and wasn't that the way life went? You had choices, you made compromises, and nothing ever went the way you expected. Adapt to survive. Stay the same and fail.

'Patrick told me your father passed away.' She hoped the admission would explain away her own outpouring. She didn't want him to think her strange. A woman who blurted out private matters to unsuspecting guests. She wasn't Radio Afloat. 'I'm sorry. It must have been awful.'

'I was fifteen and set off for school one day and when I came back, I was told he'd dropped dead. We found out later it was a brain aneurism. At least it would've been quick.'

The silence stretched between them. But it wasn't awkward. Just two people connected by tragedy. The waves lapped against the port side, and workers on the docks shouted instructions to one another.

'How come you're up so early?' she asked and resumed her sketching.

'I gave up trying to sleep with Jahmar snoring like a train.' He rubbed tired eyes. 'He always does after a skinful.'

'So other than visiting a potential movie location what else is on the agenda today?' Agnes set to work on detailing wispy clouds above a church tower.

'I don't know. But I've been told to bring swimming trunks.'

She knitted her brows. 'Don't you have any say in what happens?'

'I take it you don't know much about British stag do's?' He raised one eyebrow, as if mocking her, she gripped the pencil with annoyance. 'It's all part of the mystique. You don't know what's in store. All I know is that I have activities to complete, each one chosen by one of my mates.'

'Did Jahmar choose horse riding by any chance?' Agnes snapped.

'You don't like him much, do you?'

Agnes rounded on him. 'Do you know how unbelievably stupid and dangerous it was of him to state you were an expert? And even more ridiculous that you went along with it.'

'You're very direct, aren't you?' He was half-serious, half-teasing and didn't appear overly concerned by her outburst.

'It isn't funny, Tony,' she retorted. It was like talking to one of her teenage brothers. 'All it takes is one incident, one accident and this cruise ship will pull the horse-riding activity. Have you any idea what an extremely awkward position you put Cynthia in? If she'd confronted you about lying and it resulted in a customer complaint, she'd lose the contract. If you'd have had an accident, she'd lose the contract.'

'I didn't think about it like that,' he replied. And judging by his surprised expression she believed him. Excellent, the bloke was an idiot. Or did he simply not have the mental capacity to understand actions had consequences?

'Well, you should have.' Her pencil stabbed at the paper. 'Instead of lording it over the locals and not giving a damn about their livelihoods.'

'And here was me thinking you were just saving my life.' He grinned and she laughed. He might be a prat but at least he was an amusing one.

'Well, there was that. But if you're serious about drawing, why don't you check out the art class before dinner tonight? Vlad is our resident expert; he'll give you some pointers and it's only for an hour.'

'And talking of drawing, what's going on here, then?' He nodded at her finished masterpiece and the city. 'I know there's artistic licencing but in front of us is a bustling Italian city and you've created what appears to be a Greek fishing port.'

Her mobile vibrated and she hurriedly packed away. Where had the time gone? He dropped her music stand and handed it over. 'The picture is Corfu Town, and we dock there in eight days when you'll find out if I've done it justice.'

'Thanks, Agnes.' He held up the notepad and pencils. His smile did lend a sort of charm to his rather nondescript face. 'I'll let you know how I get on with Vlad and I look forward to feeding back my thoughts on Corfu.'

She sped along the deck, raising a hand in farewell. It was a meaningless gesture; she wouldn't see him again and he certainly wouldn't track her down with an update. It didn't matter if he liked her painting or not. Did it?

Chapter Seven

If you worked in a windowless kitchen the days merged into one another and sometimes the only way to know one day from the next was by the set menu. It was a Mediterranean cruise, so today's theme was Caribbean – go figure. As usual, the pace was hectic but at ten Agnes clocked off and, in response to a request, headed to one of the staff lounges. There were always plenty of people on a break and Agnes took a few seconds to locate the FFFC sitting in a corner watching as Vlad and Bettina argued with Rodriguez.

She slipped in next to Tomas who grinned mischievously. 'It's all kicking off tonight.'

From what she could gather, Rodriguez was attempting to dock points from the few members of the club who'd managed to attain any in the last week.

'You're deliberately sabotaging the results.' Vlad snarled. 'Rule twenty-two categorically states if a player wishes to join another player, additional points can be earned. I believe you did that three weeks ago.'

'Yes,' Bettina chimed in. 'And rule fifteen indicates if a player is tied to another club but both managers agree they can enter into a short-term agreement for extra points.'

While sitting in a crowded lounge, the club members conversed in code. Agnes still didn't know every rule inside out but grasped that the conversation concerned threesomes.

Rodriguez adjusted the collar of his lurid Hawaiian shirt. 'Neither of you have the wit to understand the subtleties of the scoring system.' He pierced a cosmopolitan-soaked morello cherry with a cocktail stick and slowly savoured it. 'Darlings, if you have nothing intelligent to contribute, have the decency to keep quiet for all our sakes.'

'I see the discussion is still ongoing,' Maria interrupted. 'So, you'll all be glad that the FFFC rules expert is on hand to settle the matter.'

Neat-as-a-pin Sebastian perched on a stool and patiently listened to each claimant. All he needed was a black cloak, a wig and a gavel. He sat digesting the news with interlaced fingers beneath his narrow chin.

'Roddy, Roddy, Roddy.' He shook his head sadly. 'Rejection is getting the better of you isn't it.'

'As usual, the man has no idea what he's talking about,' Rodriguez lazily responded. But the glass chinked against his sparkling white teeth as he downed his cocktail.

'Unsporting behaviour to protect a dwindling advantage,' Sebastian stated. 'It pains me to enact rule thirty-six.'

Rodriguez's kohl-pencilled eyes widened. 'You wouldn't dare.'

Agnes was relieved to see four confused faces; nobody else had a clue either. 'What's rule thirty-six?'

'If there is clear evidence that an FFFC member has attempted to illegally dock fellow member points, the afore mentioned individual is forthwith docked twenty points.' There was a sharp inhale around the table. 'I should clarify, that is twenty points per offence. And those points are then added on to the injured parties' scores.'

'Holy shit,' Tomas exclaimed. He sounded as if all his Christmases had come at once.

Sebastian nodded. 'It is the harshest punishment possible, apart from expulsion. By my calculations, I make that forty points from Roddy and twenty points each to Vlad and Bettina. Roddy, feel free to jump in at any time. I know you're always keen to pass judgement on my lack of arithmetic prowess.'

Maria coughed. 'Not exactly. Rodriquez also misled me about playing my joker, so I lost a clear advantage.'

'Oh dear.' Sebastian tutted. 'How the mighty have fallen.'

'It means you're dead last, Roddy.' Tomas sniggered. 'If things don't change, you'll also be scoring next season. I guess we'd better keep an eye on you to make sure there's no more cheating.'

'And it means I'm in first place,' Maria crowed. 'Just.'

A bellow of rage erupted, and in one swift movement, Rodriguez hurled the table with all their drinks and snacks across the room. It was the first time Agnes could ever recall total silence in the staff lounge. A few seconds later it was broken by a beautiful soprano voice singing 'There's No Business Like Showbusiness'. It was quickly followed by a deep baritone rendition of 'Life Is a Cabaret Old Chum'. In the far corner, a group struck up a lively version of 'Always Look on the Bright Side of Life' and then finished with a rousing 'The Eye of the Tiger'.

'Go to hell, the lot of you,' Rodriguez thundered before storming out. A ripple of laughter broke out before normal service resumed. The chatter began again, mobile phone scrolling resumed, as did an enthusiastic game of cards in the opposite corner.

'My, my. Nobody likes a sore loser,' Sebastian calmly observed and then departed with a smirk.

'That's made my year,' Tomas declared as he stood. 'Now, if you delightful people will excuse me, I'm needed on the bridge.'

Five more hurried excuses followed until only Vlad and Agnes remained surrounded by a scene of devastation.

'How come we get lumbered with tidying up?' Agnes fumed to nobody in particular as she righted the table. Vlad returned with rubbish bags, a dustpan, a brush and paper towels.

'Don't worry, it won't take long.' He quickly swept up plastic bowls, glasses, peanuts, crisps and jelly sweets. 'Credit to you, girl. Our little gallery's takings increased significantly today thanks to your two cockney mates.'

Agnes soaked up Maria's lager and squeezed the contents into a pint glass. 'I don't have two cockney mates.'

'Okay, the younger one is a born-and-bred Londoner and the older one was originally from Jamaica.' Vlad rolled his eyes as she rocked back on her heels. 'You can be *so* pedantic, sometimes. Anyway, they each bought a painting after attending my art class.'

So, Tony had dragged Patrick along. How very interesting. 'Were they any good?' she casually enquired, picking up the last few lemon pips.

They both plonked themselves down on a sofa and Vlad laughed. 'The older guy, Patrick, took it as a bit of fun and spent most of the class discussing sports cars with a chatty Welsh woman. But the younger one, Troy—'

'Tony,' Agnes corrected him.

'Sorry, Tony. Now that guy's got bags of natural talent.'

'Really?' She leaned forwards. 'Someone told him he was wasting his time, so he gave up.'

'That person was talking crap.' Vlad scrunched up a napkin and threw it in the open bin liner. 'Why do people do that? Putting others down. I'm telling you, he's got what it takes but only if he puts in the effort. And I told him so.'

'What did he say?'

'Bless, he went all shy. But his father—'

'They're not related,' she corrected him.

Vlad nodded and carried on. 'Patrick joined in and started pushing Tony to follow up with it when he got home.' He looked beyond the confines of the busy lounge and remained silent for a minute. 'I don't think he will though. I reckon the bloke lacks confidence in his own abilities.'

Agnes mulled over the information. She barely knew Tony but from the little she'd seen, he appeared to be a follower and not a leader. If his so-called mates started making fun of his interest, he'd probably give up. It made her angry, even if he wasn't her concern.

Vlad glanced at his watch. 'Sorry, Agnes, but I need to make tracks.'

'Off to score more points by any chance?' she teased.

'Too right.' He ran two fingers along his moustache and goatee. 'This is my best chance to take the title after Roddy's spectacular fall from grace.'

She was left alone on the sofa. There were plenty of people she knew chilling out. But she craved solitude and fresh air. The crew deck was far too crowded, so she set off for the top one.

Chapter Eight

The moonlight snaked across the water. They'd pulled anchor from Naples before dinner and wouldn't catch sight of their next port till the day after tomorrow. It was almost midnight and laughter from a lower deck drifted upwards to the bench she sat on. A fresh breeze and a cloudless sky filled with countless stars. What a view, what a life. She did have the most fantastic job. The chance to develop her culinary skills and enjoy spectacular locations. Yes, the hours were long, her sleeping quarters were cramped, management was a pain, there was minimal privacy, and the pay wasn't fantastic. But it would have been the same back home. No, it would have been worse, as she'd have been expected to also do all the household chores and keep an eye on her teenage brothers. The triplets were exhausting, a ready-made gang of pranksters who'd enjoyed nothing more than lying in wait to waterbomb her, hide her keys, clothes, mobile and anything else. In every other respect, they were well-behaved and hard-working; at least she'd done a good job there. Papa would have been proud of her. All things considered, life at sea was infinitely better.

A door opened and out tumbled a loved-up couple. Kissing, snuggling and cuddling were Bettina and Jahmar. At the last minute, the abrasive Londoner clocked her. No smile, no wave but a look of utter loathing. What was his problem? She leaned her head back against the ship, refusing to let him spoil her moment. The forward motion and the waves against the hull were a lullaby and her eyelids closed in response.

Running footsteps from the deck below brought her awake with a start. She fumbled for her mobile. It was quarter to one. A light, damp mist now hung over the water and its cool fingers slid beneath her coat and around her stiffening neck. She yawned and stretched in the delicious peacefulness, but her narrow bunk beckoned. Reaching for the metal door handle, she was grabbed from behind and spun around.

'Not so fast,' Jahmar snarled and with a vice-like grip he locked on to her slender wrist. 'I want a word with you.'

'Get the hell off me.' She tried to wrench her arm free, but he was far too strong. 'If you don't let go, I'll scream.'

His lips drew back to reveal perfectly white teeth. 'Go on then.' She was bluffing and he knew it. With his face centimetres from hers, the odour of musky aftershave turned her stomach. She was pinned up against the door, unable to escape. 'Keep away from Tony. He's a decent lad but easily swayed by others, so I won't have you filling his head with crap about becoming a worthless artist.'

The cold, metal door handle dug painfully into her spine, but she refused to register the pain. 'F-fuck you, Jahmar.'

He caught the tremor in her voice and sneered. 'You're nothing but a pathetic little kitchen wench who'll never amount to anything. And neither will Tony if he listens to your delusional ideas. I've invested too much time in him, I won't stand by and let him cast aside status and a well-paid career due to the misplaced ideals of a nobody. So I'm here to make sure that doesn't happen.'

'Jahmar, are you there?' Bettina's seductive voice called out from further along the deck. 'I'm getting ever so lonely here in the dark all by myself. Don't you want to come and keep me warm? I'll make it worth your while.'

'Coming, sweetheart.' His voice was light and playful but then dropped to a menacing growl. 'You've been warned. Stay away or I won't be as gentle next time.'

With a vicious twist to her arm, he stalked off. Her skin burned as she grabbed the door handle with shaking hands. Staggering inside, she slid down the wall and cradled her wrist. After several minutes, she managed to stand and scuttled back to her cabin. Crawling into the top bunk, she curled up with a battered teddy bear and pretended to be asleep when Maria crashed in sometime later.

Chapter Nine

The air was warm but Agnes shivered under the covers. The oppressive darkness pressed downwards and threatened to smother her. She frantically groped around, until beneath the squashed teddy she grasped her mobile. The dim display illuminated her narrow bunk to reveal the comforting sight of family and friends' faces tacked on the walls and ceiling. The hammering in her ribcage slowed but the I Love Corfu T-shirt clung to her clammy skin. Her spine ached and traces of overpowering aftershave lingered in her nostrils. She gingerly squeezed her wrist and winced. Painful but not unbearably so. Luckily, the intense throbbing wouldn't prevent her from working. The tears welled up again, a mixture of fear, anger and hopelessness. She couldn't report it. There was an unspoken rule – crew didn't lodge complaints against passengers. And besides, there were no witnesses. Even if she did lodge a complaint, it was a precious fare-paying guest's word against hers. And who was she? Jahmar's nasal voice whispered again; she was a nobody. Nothing but a lowly underling who'd easily be replaced. A single tear plopped onto washed-out sheets. Despite everything, she was employed by one of the most prestigious cruise companies. Their name commanded respect, so if she wanted to succeed in this business, she'd better keep her mouth shut. But for now, she craved an expansive horizon and wholesome fresh air.

It was barely light as the giant hulk of the cruise ship powered towards Valletta. Although she loved the city, Agnes did think it strange they returned to Malta for a full day. After all it was where the cruise originated and ended. But then again, most guests probably didn't get much of a chance to explore on day one or day fourteen, being ferried between the airport and ship.

With a day at sea, passengers wouldn't rush to rise early today. It was a chance to recover from relentless sightseeing agendas.

On the deserted top deck, she stepped up onto the guardrail and spread her arms wide, re-enacting a scene made famous from the blockbuster film *Titanic*. Her long brown hair streamed out behind her, and the freshness forced her to focus on the here and now.

'The mistress of all you survey.' A voice called out. 'Or should it be, I'm the empress of the world?'

She jumped down and cowered against the metal railings. 'You can't come anywhere near me.'

The man zipped up his fleece. 'Why ever not?' He didn't wait for a response or appear to notice her slowly backing away. 'You aren't an easy woman to track down. Two days in a row, I've come up here to regale you with my artistic endeavours but to no avail.' He yawned and scratched his unshaved chin. 'I must have just missed you.'

Agnes retreated further, eyes darting along the deck. 'Didn't you hear me? You must keep away. He said so.'

Again, that little boy lost look. It was quite endearing really. 'Who said that? What are you talking about?'

'Jahmar. Your best mate. He frightened me.'

And then a switch flicked. The softness around his eyes hardened. The plump, luscious lips tightened. 'What did he do?'

She rolled up her sleeve to reveal a hand-sized bruise and he cautiously stepped forward in the pre-dawn light. 'I-I have to keep away from you and … and stop filling your head with r-ridiculous ideas about becoming an artist.'

'Oh, Agnes.'

And that did it. Undone by kindness. Why couldn't he have stayed angry? She could have held it together. But no, he had to be kind and concerned. And that's what he was still doing. Asking her to explain it all, as best she could. And out it all tumbled, in a snotty, sobbing torrent of heaving shoulders and stuttering words. Thank God she wasn't trying to impress him. In two strides he was there, cocooning her in surprisingly strong arms. He was fractionally taller, but their bodies clicked into place, like jigsaw pieces. She buried into his chest and liked the weight of his chin resting comfortably on her head. His fleece was soon soaked and despite wanting to stay, she pulled away and snuffled an apology. The man even had a neatly pressed handkerchief which she gratefully honked into.

'Don't you dare apologise for an arsehole hurting you.'

'Papa would have said the same thing.' She blew her nose one last time and self-consciously stuffed it up her sleeve. 'I'll get that back to you once it's clean.'

He shook his head. 'Don't be ridiculous. Keep it. It's the least I can do. Your father was a smart bloke.'

'In some ways, yes. He was the best. In other ways, not at all.' She turned towards the horizon and watched as first light flickered along it. Nature in all her glory. But it didn't fill her with joy. Today there was nothing but a yearning for what could never be. 'He left me,' she whispered. 'I can't believe Papa left me.'

Standing beside her, Tony gently squeezed her hand. 'I get angry sometimes at my dad for not being here. How his death forced me to change the course of my life. He was gone and suddenly there were all these creditors demanding immediate payment. Dad had been up to his eyes in debt … the prestigious job, my private education, our beautiful house, and the high-end cars … it all came crashing down. Luckily, Jahmar's father put in a good word for me, and I secured an IT apprenticeship. So, I didn't get to do what I wanted to do, but I did what I could and what was best for my family, what would help to pay the bills. I hate him for that. And then I'm overcome with guilt at my selfishness and then I'm left incredibly sad. It's a perpetual circle that I can't break.'

He moved away and sat on a bench. Agnes joined him. Her father's death had intensified that unshakeable desire to be a chef. And the knowledge that life could be ripped out from under you had spurred her on. Unlike Tony, she was selfish in putting her ambition above everything else. She'd left her family, her friends and her long-term boyfriend to pursue a goal. Tony had done the complete opposite. He was the honourable one. Not her. So much for thinking she was better than him.

She raked her windswept hair back into a tight bun. 'I guess we make the most of the time we're given. However long that is.'

The dawn sky helped to soothe away some of her fears, but she hated to admit it. Jahmar had scared her, badly. And they weren't even halfway through the cruise yet. Perhaps it might be best if she stuck to the staff areas. Yes, that was a good idea. She chewed a fingernail and frowned. But that would mean bowing down to a bully, and the top deck was hers. Why should she be forced to cower beneath stairs? She had as much right to be up here as anybody else. And it had nothing to do with a certain groom-to-be frequenting the area. No, he was off limits. She wasn't going there. She wasn't Rodriguez.

'Agnes?' His voice was gentle, kind and caring. It was a lovely voice. A voice you'd like to wake up to in the morning. Did he bring his fiancée breakfast in bed? Tony in bed … she mentally shook the image out of her head. Why had that popped in there? He was studying her now. Could he mindread? Heat radiated up her neck. 'Are you okay? Do you want me to go and fetch someone? Maybe Maria?'

He was concerned, that was nice to know. 'No, I'm fine. My emotional outburst and the fresh air have helped.'

His eyes strayed to the door. 'Are you sure? You don't look quite right.' He hastily raised both hands. 'No, I-I didn't mean that. You look great. What I should have said … what I was trying to say—'

'I'm fine, Tony.' How funny for him to be tongue-tied. And for him to think she looked great with bloodshot eyes, a snotty nose and greasy hair. She unzipped her coat to cool down. It was never usually this warm. They must be going through a hotspot, one of those weird maritime anomalies she'd read about. Okay, who was she kidding, she'd never read anything of the sort. She looked at the deck, at the horizon, anywhere but his soulful eyes.

‘Okay, if you’re absolutely sure?’ She mutely nodded with eyes downcast. ‘Then it’s time for me to go and have a word with my best mate.’

‘What!’ She straightened. ‘It’s barely five a.m.’

‘I don’t give a shit what time it is.’ There was an intensity to his face she’d never seen before. ‘Nobody has the right to terrify someone else. And he sure as hell isn’t determining my future.’

‘I-I don’t know what to say. I—’

‘You thought I wouldn’t confront him, didn’t you?’ He wasn’t angry but the sadness in his voice threatened to set her off again.

‘You look different somehow,’ she whispered. That was the trick, keep the voice low and it held her tears in check. ‘You don’t look like—’

‘A pushover,’ he supplied and retreated into himself. He barely seemed to fill his five-foot-ten frame. ‘All my life I’ve done what was expected or what I’ve been told to do. It didn’t matter if I didn’t agree. I’d remain silent, even in the face of inappropriate behaviour. Or even worse I’d join in and then secretly apologise later, just like I did with Maria.’ His deflating body continued to fold inwards, and Agnes realised she was holding her breath. ‘I’ve been a coward. But not anymore. You have my word; Jahmar will never come anywhere near you again.’

And now he was standing tall, defiant, and proud. He would keep his word. He would protect her. The sense of relief was overwhelming. But this time when her tear ducts filled, she refused to let them overflow.

‘Thank you, Tony.’

He gave a tight smile. ‘No, thank *you*.’

Chapter Ten

At the end of her shift, Agnes scuttled back to the safety of her cabin. Even with Tony's reassurances, she was still on edge. Tacked to her bunk was a note.

Meet me in the spa when you've finished work. Don't even think about ignoring this message. Maria x

Fifteen minutes later, Agnes pushed open gleaming glass doors to find her friend chatting to the immaculately presented Radio Afloat. And unsurprisingly, the young beautician was midway through broadcasting cruise-ship gossip. Bettina had been spot on. Vlad's jilted lover would blab to anyone and everyone about any juicy titbit. Agnes fidgeted uncomfortably in her baggy T-shirt and combat pants. Her hair was still damp, and she didn't have on a scrap of makeup. The two women opposite epitomised style and grace. Even after a full shift, they both oozed sophistication. It was clearly a beautiful-person thing which, try as she might, Agnes couldn't emulate. The meditative music, warm air and lavender aroma lulled her into a dreamlike state. She could easily fall asleep.

'How do you stay awake?' she muttered and lay her head on the cool marble counter.

'Enough of that, young lady.' Maria took her by the arm. 'Come with me.'

There was a mischievous glint in her friend's eyes as she steered Agnes towards a door. 'I hope you've got your dancing shoes on.'

Inside the studio were ten couples of assorted shapes and ages. And two partnerless men: Tony and Patrick.

'Just in time,' Bettina declared. 'Agnes, you're with Tony and Maria is with Patrick.'

Tony smiled sheepishly and held out his hand. 'Fancy a salsa?'

'I-I can't.' This was a nightmare. She couldn't dance. She never danced. 'I don't know how. I don't know what to do.' It didn't help that Maria was being playfully dipped by Patrick.

'Don't look so terrified,' Bettina murmured as she breezed past, going to the rescue of a tweed-attired Scottish couple who looked more suited to the golf course than a dance class. 'Gentlemen, only one of you can lead.'

Tony placed his hand lightly on her waist. 'Don't worry, I've been dragged along to a salsa club for the last three years by my sisters.'

'So, I take it this isn't a beginner's class?' Agnes watched as couples effortlessly glided and twisted around the parquet floor.

'Erm, no—'

She was breaking into a cold sweat. This was going to be horrific. Tony could be a world-champion salsa dancer and it wouldn't make a difference as she had no clue. It would only highlight her gross lack of talent. She tried to pull away from him, but he tightened his grip. The panic was rising, and she couldn't get enough oxygen into her lungs.

'Okay, ladies and gentlemen. As this is advanced salsa appreciation, I won't waste any time going over the steps. However, I will be coming around to give guidance and encouragement,' Bettina instructed. 'Now, let's get dancing.'

'I'm going to be sick.' The room was swirling. Thrown in at the deep end was not how she operated. She stuck to what she was good at and then built on that. 'I'm going to faint. I'll make a complete idiot of myself. I'm going to completely embarrass you. It'll be hell for both of us. I should leave.'

But all he did was laugh, and it was warm and friendly. 'You'll be fine, just follow my lead.'

They set off and she didn't collapse instantly into a jabbering heap. She didn't trip over her feet, or his, and she didn't throw up or black out. Instead, she gained in confidence because he was a self-assured dancer.

‘I think I’m getting the hang of this,’ she muttered ten minutes later with her eyes glued to the floor.

‘Don’t look down.’ His thumb and forefinger gently tilted her chin upwards. ‘You’re a natural, kid.’

She’d never noticed what gorgeous eyelashes he had. Or the rather cute dimple in his chin. Her stomach churned and it wasn’t because she hadn’t eaten for ten hours.

‘Excellent hip movement, Agnes,’ Bettina commented. ‘Patrick, that’s jive, not salsa.’

There was a whoop as Maria sailed skywards and then shot through her partner’s legs.

Thirty minutes later, Agnes was no longer repeating the steps in her head. His arm rested comfortably on her waist as she was filled with the most amazing sense of joy. She’d always avoided dancing at all costs, having been teased since childhood for being tall and gangly. Her ex hadn’t helped either. On the odd occasion they’d stepped onto a dancefloor he’d held her at arm’s length like an unexploded bomb. Neither had enjoyed the experience.

Time rolled backwards and she was a six-year-old bridesmaid at her father and stepmother’s wedding. They’d been so much in love and with eyes only for each other had glided around the dancefloor. She’d sat cross-legged on the ground and watched them twirl and swirl beneath fairy lights and a star-studded sky. At any family gathering, they were always the first up and the last to sit back down.

But after her father was killed, her stepmother refused to dance again. And for the first time, Agnes realised just how hard it must have been for the woman she called Mama to lose her soulmate and be left to raise four children. She cringed at all the teenage strops she’d thrown at being forced to care for her brothers. All her exhausted stepmother wanted was a rest, but Agnes made that as difficult as possible and then flitted off to work at sea. What a bitch. And wasn’t that the last comment her long-term boyfriend had messaged her with? Dumped after six years by text. He’d messaged to say she was an ambitious bitch who would go far. Conversely, he hadn't needed to go far at all. A week later (so she discovered) he'd hooked up with her best mate. They were now married with a kid on the way. Another reason to avoid home.

'Why the serious face?' Tony probed. 'Aren't you enjoying the class?'

'Sorry.' She snapped back to the present. 'I'm having a great time. I was just thinking I've never danced with anyone before who didn't step on my toes.'

He half-smiled. 'What else? If you're still worried about Jahmar, don't be. It's all sorted.'

'What happened?' Now that he'd brought up the topic, Agnes was keen to find out how the confrontation had gone.

'Patrick, that's flamenco.' The rather exasperated voice of Bettina drifted across the studio, followed by Maria's laughter.

'Well, I can truly say it's the first time I've seen my soon-to-be brother-in-law speechless.'

Agnes nearly collided into Patrick and Maria. 'Your fiancée is your best mate's sister?'

He laughed and effortlessly steered them away from the waltzing couple. 'Oh yes, Jahmar made it happen. He knew I had a soft spot for his baby sister but that I'd never do anything about it.'

'And why not?' Agnes demanded. 'Why would she say no to you?'

'Because she was way out of my league,' Tony replied. 'She was far and away the most popular, the best-looking girl in school and from the poshest part of town.'

Agnes had visions of a stuck-up, spoilt princess in designer gear. She hated her instantly. 'Well, you must have done something right. I mean, you're getting married.' He smiled but she noticed it didn't reach his eyes.

'Anyway, back to your first question.' Was it her imagination or had he skilfully changed the subject? 'I kicked off big style and said I didn't care if he had more money than the rest of the stag do put together. Did he think that gave him the right to terrify people? Did it give him the right to dictate my life? As far as I was concerned, he could go to hell and although it'd take time, I'd pay him back ever damned penny of the holiday. I wasn't going to be in his debt. And I didn't give a toss if he blabbed to his sister either. She'd have to deal with me earning less when I went to art school. It was about time she pulled her weight and perhaps spent her own money for once instead of living off everyone else.'

'Tony, you're going to make Agnes sick if you don't slow down,' Bettina called from across the room.

And indeed, the more he'd talked, the faster the room had spun. His hand loosened its grip on hers as their speed lessened. 'Sorry about that.'

She closed her eyes briefly to refocus. But the comment about his fiancée leeching off others lingered. Why did it give her a sense of smug satisfaction that her initial assessment had been right? The woman was obviously a parasite, living off her fiancé, brother and parents.

'That's okay,' she replied. 'What happened then?'

'Patrick, could you attempt to do at least one salsa move?' Bettina's voice pleaded. The maverick couple now appeared to be line dancing.

'Jahmar got out of bed to give me a standing ovation and said it was about time I finally located my balls and stood up for myself. He sends his deepest apologies and realises he was bang out of order. He also said I could give his sister the good news and seemed thoroughly amused at the idea.'

'And you're going to art school?' Agnes beamed. 'That's brilliant news. I'm so excited for you.'

His smile was a mixture of embarrassment and pride. 'I've already contacted a few places. I'm going to have to do a foundation course first, which has already started. But they've asked me to send in some samples. If they like my work, I might be able to join. But if not, I'll do some online courses until next September.'

The music stopped but the giggles and chatter continued. 'Fantastic job, everyone.' Bettina's voice rose above the noise. 'Give yourselves a round of applause. Especially Patrick and Maria who managed to incorporate six different dance styles into a salsa class.'

But instead of clapping, Agnes threw her arms around Tony. 'I'm so proud of you.'

'Thanks. You don't know what that means.'

He swung her around and she let out a whoop, far louder than any of Maria's.

Chapter Eleven

After high fiving everyone in the group, Patrick linked arms with Maria and Agnes. 'Come on ladies, let's get something to eat. I'm famished.'

Agnes glanced at Maria who nodded. 'We'd be delighted.'

It was after ten but on a cruise ship you could eat around the clock. Maria and Agnes slid into an American-style diner booth as the blokes stood at the counter pondering over a selection of burgers, chilli con carne, chicken chow mein, pizza and enchiladas.

'Are you sure we're okay to be here?' Agnes asked and furtively scanned the room for any managers who might swoop down and drag her away.

Maria waved a pain au chocolat in the air. 'You worry too much. We've been invited by guests, so it's fine.'

'Thanks for organising the salsa class. It was just what I needed.' Agnes sipped her strawberry milkshake. She hadn't told her friend about last night's events. Maria had still been flat out in the morning when Agnes returned to the cabin. And now, she saw no point in raking things up.

Her friend glanced over to where the two men were busy quizzing the chef about a chilli con carne pizza. 'I know what happened with Jahmar. Why didn't you tell me?' Maria's voice reflected both anger and hurt.

Agnes stirred her drink. 'You'd had a late night and looked so peaceful. I didn't want to wake you up and pour out my tale of woe.' Maria savagely dunked her pastry into her glass, causing a tidal wave of milky coffee to slop over the table. Agnes quickly mopped it up. 'Sorry, I should have said something.'

'Yes, you should have,' Maria hissed. 'Instead, I had to hear it from Tony. Do you know how stupid I felt? My best friend won't tell me she's been terrified out of her wits but tells a virtual stranger.'

'It-it wasn't like that,' Agnes tried to explain but Maria silenced her with a fierce stare.

'The bloke was worried about you. I don't know how long it must have taken him to track me down on the ship.'

'Really?' Agnes's cheeks burned. 'I told him I was fine. He should have kept quiet.'

'Stop being so affronted,' Maria snapped. 'There's nothing wrong in somebody watching out for you. Don't you think it's nice, what he did? And I'm not just talking about him telling me about Jahmar being an arse. Don't you realise it was Tony's idea about the dancing? Not mine. He thought it might cheer you up.'

'I'm not saying it's not lovely,' Agnes replied hesitantly. She couldn't think straight. He had taken time out from his holiday to cheer her up. 'It's just that I …' She trailed off, not knowing how to finish.

Maria smirked. 'I think somebody is developing a little bit of a crush on one of the passengers.'

'Will you shut up,' Agnes hissed as the two men made their way across to them. 'He's engaged to be married.'

Maria held her hands up in parley. 'Sorry. All I'm saying is it took a full year before I was rewarded with a hug. Yet, you've known Monsieur Acebi less than eight days, and he gets one.'

Agnes threw daggers at her friend, who simply smiled.

Chapter Twelve

When Tony looked back on the day, it could only be described as a weird one. Their group had been the first to disembark. Jahmar had almost exploded with rage as the crew held them back until the gangway was secured. His best mate announced that if their group was not on the quayside in ten minutes flat, he was going to report every crew member to the captain who he'd had the pleasure of dining with for the last five nights. That got a rocket up their backsides. And Jahmar was like that. His utter confidence meant that people fell into line. He also had a built-in radar for locating the most powerful, richest or important person in any situation and then striking up a conversation.

Tony was the complete opposite. He sometimes wondered how on earth they'd remained friends, and on one drunken night out had asked why Jahmar was his mate. He'd been clapped on the back and informed it was because he kept the playboy grounded.

For movie buffs, Malta was a dream. Not only had two James Bond films featured on the island but it seemed impossible to go anywhere (especially in Valletta) without tripping over a Hollywood blockbuster location – Gladiator, Troy, The Count of Monte Cristo and Midnight Express to name a few. And then there was Popeye village – a wonderful wacky place.

It had been a jam-packed itinerary and their taxi driver had driven like a man possessed to get them back to the ship. They'd been pulling the gangway in as their minibus screeched to a halt. Talk about cutting it fine. And throughout the day, Jahmar had been off-key, constantly checking his mobile, sending messages and repeatedly quizzing Tony about Bettina. What had he told her about the incident with Agnes? The man wouldn't let up, convinced Tony was holding out on him. In the end, Tony had let rip at being falsely accused. It felt good, standing up for himself, and Jahmar had backed off. He hadn't even seen the woman and certainly wouldn't have said anything to her. And all because the dance teacher was blanking Jahmar, which never happened to the bloke. Welcome to the real world, Tony was tempted to say. But females had always flocked to his charismatic friend, who could turn on the charm, seduce them and then drop them like unwanted, dirty laundry. The tables had been well and truly turned this time and Jahmar couldn't handle it. Was it wrong to be happy that his mate was getting his just desserts?

Tony's conscience was clear in so far as he hadn't told Bettina directly. But he had told Maria, who'd almost dropped her extremely expensive camera overboard in shock. He couldn't keep the news to himself because, despite Agnes's protestations, she was clearly not fine. The woman was in a hell of a state, and he'd been loath to leave her and have it out with the colossal prick that was Jahmar. He couldn't comprehend the man's behaviour. Who would do such a thing? You didn't go around threatening people because they were giving encouragement and good advice to somebody else. It made him question if he knew his mate after all. Yes, Jahmar had a temper and was used to getting his own way, but there were some things you just didn't do. Maria must have told Bettina. There was no other explanation. And secretly Tony was pleased. It would serve Jahmar right if Bettina dumped him.

It wasn't only Jahmar who was acting strangely. Patrick was also distracted. He wasn't angry but edgy, as if he was waiting for news. When Tony asked if everything was okay, he was told not to worry. Patrick was trying to sort out a cock-up with his work roster. The idiots had put him down to work on Tony's wedding and he was in the process of sorting it out. Tony was relieved. He needed Patrick to be there and bear witness to the most important and happiest day in his life.

And that brought him nicely to his fiancée and the post-lunch incident, which Tony was still unable to forgive. The group had stopped at a café next to the rugged Maltese coastline and as their minibus driver took a ten-minute cigarette break and the others plotted the next stag task, Tony rang home. He wanted to check everything was okay with his girls; scrolling through countless photos wasn't the same thing.

Last summer, he'd arrived at work (or the chicken pen as he called it) on a swelteringly hot day. With broken air con, all the windows were wide open in the hopes of catching a slight breeze. Sweating indoors, he'd become aware of constant mewing. His fellow battery hens appeared oblivious, eyes forward while downing cans of lukewarm pop. They merely shrugged at his enquiries; it wasn't any of their concern. He'd gone outside and followed the plaintive cries to a cardboard box next to the bins. As he peered inside, three sets of eyes locked onto his. They belonged to a trio of tiny black and tan balls of fluff. It was love at first sight. He'd apprehensively brought the kittens home and unbelievably been granted permission to not only keep them (if he took sole charge) but to name them.

As he cooed over Moneypenny, Thunderball and Dr. No, his fiancée quickly pointed out that he was a natural father. And he instantly understood – that was why the kittens could stay. To support her argument about having kids sooner rather than later. It wasn't that he didn't want them – he adored his nieces and nephews – but he couldn't see the rush. He'd delayed proposing as long as possible, knowing the minute he did it would kick-start Operation Wedding of the Century and once concluded it would then trigger Operation Having Children.

He'd already been informed that while pregnant with their first child, she would be leaving work and probably wouldn't consider going back until the youngest (they were going to have four) was off to university. And probably then it would be part-time. Tony wasn't fooled. She would leave work never to return. She'd emulate her mother, who filled her time with gym classes, golf, shopping sprees, lunches with the girls, multiple holidays and fundraising. And all that was fine because her mother was rich. Conversely, they (and that meant him) were nowhere near being multi-millionaires. He was going to be skint for the rest of his life. And that was even before he'd broken the news about becoming an art student.

Penny, Thunder, and Doc had been timid and terrified at first. They'd hidden under the spare bed for a fortnight, only coming out for food and to be placed in the litter tray. And then bit by bit they learned to trust him and seek him out for affection. He was the head of the pride, and they'd trot around the house in his wake or curl up with him on the sofa. They gave him their unconditional love as he did in return. Sasha endured them. And in turn, they wisely skirted around the chief lioness. Needless to say, he'd been apprehensive about leaving them in her care, but he'd received short shift at even suggesting his mum would take them. He was informed that Sasha was perfectly capable of caring for them. They were cats – how difficult could it be? So, against his better judgement, he'd relented, but over the holiday his unease grew. She'd told him there was no need to call, she'd be too busy with wedding preparations, so an occasional message would suffice.

Today was Thursday. She'd be working from home but nonetheless, he rang with the usual nervousness. Would he receive a tongue-lashing for calling against orders or conversely for not ringing until now? He knew not to ring if she was in the office. That was a big no-no. However, her phone rang and rang, which was highly unusual. It was an additional limb, always with her. He was on the point of disconnecting when it was finally answered. But not by his fiancée.

Chapter Thirteen

At first, he was totally thrown by the shiny, heavily made-up face appearing on screen. But then he realised it was one of her friends, the rail-thin one who monitored his every move with beady eyes and squinted down her stub nose at him. That is unless she wanted help with her home computer or mobile phone. Sasha always loved informing everyone what a wonder at IT he was and in turn he was expected to fix all her friends' technology issues. He learned to stayed firmly upstairs with the cats but spent all night responding to requests shouted from the living room to 'pop to the shops, darling, we've run out of prosecco', 'can you nip out again, sweetheart, and pick up some snacks?' and 'I hate to do this, baby, but could you go and pick up our takeaway? I would go, but I've had a drink'. Thankfully, his fiancée preferred to do her socialising outside their home, which he preferred. But all it meant was she'd return home with an instruction to 'go and collect such and such's computer from the boot, sweetheart. I said you'd work your magic'. And of course, he'd do it. My God, he was a doormat.

He'd had to shout at half-cut rodent woman to be heard over salsa music blasting out of some Cuban-themed bar. Through much slurring he eventually understood that a group of them were at a three-day dance event in Bristol he knew nothing about. And not only that, but Miss Shrew also let slip they all frequented a salsa bar each Tuesday night. After much giggling, the call was disconnected, and he'd been unable to get through again.

What the hell was going on? She'd always complained they didn't do enough together, hated him going to salsa but wouldn't go because she despised his sisters. And here she was, not only lying to him about her Tuesday movie night in with friends, but she had also abandoned his girls. And if she wasn't looking after them, who was? It wouldn't be his mum or sisters, who had as little to do with his wife-to-be as possible. Jahmar claimed to know nothing about the trip and his parents wouldn't have the cats either as they had four highly territorial guard dogs. He couldn't ring any of the neighbours as he didn't have their numbers. He was on friendly enough terms with them but there was no love lost between them and his fiancée. She made it clear to them that they were beneath her. Absolutely distraught, he'd had no other option but to ring his mum in tears and ask her to go around and report back.

Until then, he headed up to the top deck in the hopes of seeing Agnes but was disappointed not to find her. It was late, and people milled around on deck, watching the ship being cast off from the dock. He was alone. Jahmar and Patrick had mumbled excuses about needing to make some calls. And the rest of the lads were grabbing a late supper before a few games of cards in the Mariners cocktail lounge. Why did they all want to miss this spectacle? Valletta looked magnificent, its walls lit up in the darkness. It should have been a wonderful day, but his stomach churned. He'd not eaten a thing since lunch time. His phone buzzed and he quickly rang his mum back, stuff the cost. She was cagey at first, saying his girls were fine but she was taking them back to hers until he returned. But he could hear that undercurrent in her voice when she was mad but didn't want to say anything. In other words, most of the time she was in the same room as his fiancée.

He wouldn't give up till she gave a full account. His poor girls had been confined to the tiny kitchen and adjoining garage. The cat flap had been locked shut so they'd had no access to outside and with the rest of the house off limits to them, they'd been forced to sleep on either a hard wooden or concrete floor. Their congealed food was untouched, and their water bowl was empty. They'd been huddled together, crying at the back door when his mum walked in and she'd spent the next hour cleaning up, feeding and watering them before they demanded lots of cuddles on the sofa. The tears slid down his face as he thanked his mum repeatedly, before eventually she pleaded for him to hang up as she had an early start the next day.

He switched off his phone and watched another port slip from view. His head throbbed with rage and shame at forcing his mum to drive over after a twelve-hour shift and then cat sit because his fiancée was a selfish cow. This was the worst thing to date. She wanted to be a mother but thought nothing of vanishing without a trace and shirking her responsibilities to his gorgeous girls. He gripped the guardrail tightly and breathed deeply to calm down. Luckily, tomorrow was a day at sea, so no early start. This sightseeing gig was trashing.

People gradually retreated indoors but he remained until he eventually realised Agnes wasn't going to appear. And hadn't he come to the top deck for that very reason? A wave of despondency washed over him. Why was he bothered? He didn't want to answer the question. He knew so little about the rather abrasive, stern-looking Greek chef. In fact, he didn't even know if that was her job. He didn't know her surname, her age or where she'd grown up. So, what did he know about her?

He knew she'd lost her father and hadn't got over it. She loved cooking and liked drawing. She was an accomplished equestrian but didn't watch movies. She didn't like the thought of people laughing at her or trying something new. But she had enjoyed dancing with him, and a smile twitched around his mouth. She'd said she was proud of him for following his artistic dream and she gave great hugs. He sank down onto the very bench they'd sat on a few days ago. And wasn't that the problem? He felt more connected to a woman he barely knew than the woman he was due to marry. And he might as well admit that he missed his cats more than his fiancée. And how much did his wife-to-be care about him? When was the last time she'd said 'I love you'? Frighteningly, he couldn't remember. That couldn't be good surely. He was twenty-eight and the first one of his mates to get married. They'd all laughed and said rather him than them. So why was he getting married? Because it was what you did. Go to school, fall in love, get a job, get a car, get a house, get married and have kids. The order might switch around but wasn't that what most of the world's population aspired to? Shouldn't he be grateful for what he had? Wasn't it enough? The questions buffeted around his mind until he finally gave up and went to see if his mates were still up.

Chapter Fourteen

A day at sea and another day in the kitchen.

Agnes lay on her bunk and stared at the photos of friends and family. It was five a.m. but there was no need to go on deck. She'd done that last night. After another ludicrously busy day, made worse by two colleagues laid up with some stomach bug, she'd gone to the staff deck. Why would she want to go to the top deck? She didn't need to see Tony. She didn't have a crush on him. No matter what Maria said. She'd watched the minibus squeal to a stop and seen him and his mates pelt along the quayside, yelling at the jeering crew to hold the gangway. Everyone was hanging over the guardrails, cheering them on. It was a participation event and passengers and crew loved to witness just how close people came to missing the boat. Tony's group was the nearest yet. Not that they would have left without them. Tony had hit the gangway first which was hardly surprising. He kept himself in shape, she knew that from their salsa class. The way his hands had guided her, the way his slim hips had moved, the way he held her eyes. She kicked off the covers. It was getting far too hot in the cabin.

Her mind strayed back to the previous night. Patrick was by far the oldest, but he boarded in second place. And begrudgingly Agnes had to hand it to Jahmar, he'd waited on the quayside until a rather rotund member of the group staggered onto the ramp. He'd then air-kissed the cheering crowds. She'd spent the rest of the evening chatting with various people, sketching and finally writing a letter home she'd been meaning to do for weeks. She had kept herself busy last night, so there was no opportunity to see Tony.

She plonked teddy on her chest. Usually, he sat on a shelf as a good luck mascot, but since the incident with Jahmar, he'd cuddled up next to her.

'I'm not going,' she whispered.

He stared back.

'No, I'm not a coward.'

The bear remained silent in his handknitted cardigan. Judging her.

'What would you know about it anyway? You're only stuffed with fluff.' She hurled him down the end of the bunk. His head hit the wall and she immediately sprung up and hugged him. 'I'm sorry.'

'Will you stop having a conversation with an inanimate object and go back to sleep?' Maria's amused voice sounded in the darkness. 'Or go up and see Tony, which is what we both know you want to do.'

'It is not.'

'It is so.'

'Okay, fine. Just to shut you up, I'll take a wander upstairs. But he's unlikely to be there.'

'Mais oui, mademoiselle,' came the sleepy response before gentle breathing.

Chapter Fifteen

Agnes paused in the corridor to catch her breath before turning the handle and casually strolling onto the empty deck. It was the fresh air, that's why she was here. Yes, that was the reason. She pulled her wool hat down over her ears to keep out the cool breeze and set off along the port side, around the stern and was scanning the starboard side when a squeak made her turn excitedly. A runner pounded past with a cheery hello. She managed a glum response, watched him disappear, and set off again.

'I thought you'd be a morning person.' She spun around and there he was, unshaven, with messy hair and appearing utterly wrecked. But joy surged through her entire body, and she broke into a broad grin at him holding aloft coffee and croissants. 'I think I need these more than you.'

They sat down on their bench. Was that right to call it their bench, she wondered, and gratefully accepted an early breakfast. 'You're a prince among men, Mr Acebi.'

He nodded graciously. 'And what's your surname? I realised last night I didn't know.'

'Karapetsa.' Her heart rate accelerated. So he'd been thinking about her. Had she stolen into his dreams, into his bed? She ripped off her hat. It was also far too hot outside.

'And whereabouts in Greece did you grow up? Somewhere stunningly beautiful, overlooking the sea?' he asked wistfully.

'Not exactly. I grew up in northern Greece, in a town called Kato Nevrokopi which you won't have heard of.' He shook his head. 'It's close to the Bulgarian border, gets extremely chilly in winter and is about eighty kilometres from the sea.'

'So, you didn't grow up sunning yourself in a bikini on the beach?'

She choked on her coffee but quickly recovered. 'Would you like to see that?'

'I imagine there's a special somebody in Kato Nevrokopi who'd enjoy that?' He was staring at her intently as he bit into his almond croissant.

Could he hear her heart hammering away? She kept her voice level. 'Oh no, not there or anywhere else. I'm not as lucky as you.'

'Why haven't you brought your sketch pad?'

Again, she noticed how he tactfully changed the subject, which seemed weird. Shouldn't he be singing his fiancée's praises? Or was this cruise one last fling before he tied the knot? He certainly wouldn't be the first or the last. His mate Jahmar certainly liked the ladies and Patrick was a flirt, but Agnes got the impression that he and the rest of his mates weren't like that. They were harmless, a group of lads who liked films.

'No, I thought I'd give it a miss this morning. How about you?'

He bounced up and down on the bench and presented his notepad for inspection. 'Give me your honest opinion. I was up most of last night and I'm going to do more today. I want to have a good selection to send off next week when I get back home.'

She used the napkin to clean icing sugar from her fingers before taking the notepad from his shaking hands. Bless, he was nervous. In a relatively short space of time, he'd produced an assortment of sketches and as she flicked through the pages the pencil strokes gained in confidence. The same eyes, nose and lips and then the same woman's face. She ran her fingers over the intricate detailing of braided hair framing a proud face, and then across challenging eyes and over a flawless complexion. This must be his fiancée.

'My God, she's stunning.' Of course, she would be. Beautiful and bold. And probably amazingly talented too. A prime candidate for FFFC membership. But that was cruel. This was the face of somebody in love. Agnes shifted uncomfortably, so what was she doing here? She continued to flick through the rest of the notepad and there were pages of cats in various poses.

'Who are these cuties?' They reminded her of some of the strays her papa had fed after closing time at the restaurant. Her stepmother had constantly complained at him for encouraging them. But after he died, she'd continued to go out the back with scraps and they'd flocked to her.

His eyes lit up. 'Those are Moneypenny, Thunderball and Dr. No. They're my girls, we're a mini pride.'

Interesting how he'd referred to them as his and not theirs. Maybe he'd had them before they moved in together. Or maybe him and his fiancée didn't live together? Maybe they came from very religious families? It underlined how little she knew about him.

'If I'm not mistaken, those are names from James Bond films.'

He gave her a sly smile. 'Have you been swotting up?'

'Maybe.'

They held each other's eyes for a few seconds before he coughed and pointed at his sketch pad. 'Anyway … what do y-you think?' He so wanted her approval, and she didn't understand why he was so apprehensive. Couldn't he see what she could? 'Tony, these are amazing. The shading, the composition, the intensity. Vlad was right, you've got so much natural talent. You must develop it. And your fiancée, she's going to love them.'

'Do you really think so?' He leaned back against the ship and studied the picture anew. 'I've been looking at them so long that I can't see them anymore. If that makes any sense.'

Agnes tilted her head and studied the picture again. The words almost stuck in her throat. 'When do you get married?'

'Later this month. It's going to be in her parents' back garden.' He fidgeted in his seat. 'It's more like the lawn of a stately home and there'll be a huge marquee for all the guests. We hope the ceremony will be outside, but in October who knows. It could be glorious or it could chuck it down.'

'Either way, you must be excited to have all your friends and family there?' She didn't want to know, but it would appear rude not to enquire about what was to be the happiest day of his life.

He smiled but it seemed a bit sad. He was probably thinking about his father. 'I bet you'll have a fantastic day.'

Tony gave a determined nod. 'Yes, it will be wonderful, won't it? Because if you love somebody you have to accept the good and the bad, don't you? I mean nobody's perfect, are they? And everybody makes mistakes, don't they?'

What a bizarre thing to say. It was as if he was continuing a conversation she wasn't privy to, and she had no idea how to respond. 'Erm, I suppose so.'

'Can I ask you to appraise my other drawings tonight?' He closed the notepad, stowed it away in his manbag and appeared not to have heard her reply. 'I trust your opinion and don't have anyone else I feel comfortable asking. I can ask Patrick, but he'll say anything I do is fantastic. The man is totally biased.'

Agnes wasn't entirely sure she fell into the unbiased camp either but nodded and declared she'd be honoured. He needed a confidence boost, though heavens knew why. Anyone with the use of their eyes could see how good he was.

'Why don't you show them to Vlad? I know he'd love them, and he'll be able to provide much better feedback than me.'

'I think for now, I'll stick with you. If that's okay?' Heat flared across her cheeks. Why was she blushing? This was ridiculous behaviour. He glanced at his watch. 'Isn't it time for you to make tracks?'

'Crap, I'd better fly.'

She sprinted along the deck and wrenched open the door before tearing along the corridor. A door opened ahead, and she skidded to a halt. It was Jahmar. She frantically scanned for a hiding place and slipped into a cleaner's cupboard just as Bettina appeared.

'I want a word with you,' his voice sneered, and Agnes could visualise the scene as she leaned against a collection of mops.

Footsteps approached and stopped right outside. Agnes held her breath; she didn't want to eavesdrop but didn't have much choice. And she would have to make her presence known if things turned nasty. Not that Bettina sounded ruffled as she patiently explained why she was unable to continue a relationship with a man who'd threatened her friend. He was demanding to know who had gossiped but Bettina refused to break a confidence. The usual bolshiness was gone, and he was begging her to reconsider, that he knew how wrong he'd been and that it would never happen again.

'Do you see this?' Inside the cupboard, Agnes had no idea what Bettina was showing him. 'I got it from a boyfriend who kept promising me his violence would stop. But it never did. I hope you mean what you say, Jahmar, but I'm sorry, I won't take that risk again.'

The silence stretched out and Agnes wanted to scream for them to wrap it up. She was going to be late.

'You were average at best.' The sentence dripped with venom, but Bettina only laughed.

'It'll be easy for you to move on and forget all about me then.'

'I already have,' he hissed.

Their footsteps retreated and Agnes heard a door slam. It was all quiet and she slipped out to find the acoustics had tricked her. Standing drained of colour was Bettina. She held up three misshapen fingers on her left hand. How had Agnes never noticed before?

'I'm so sorry, Bettina. I never knew.'

'They were repeatedly slammed in a kitchen drawer because he refused to believe I'd been held up at work. I then had to make his supper, tidy the flat and then … and then I-I had to—'

Agnes held up her hands. She didn't want to know. 'You don't have to tell me.'

'It's why I play the game,' Bettina responded calmly. She'd already corked her emotions. 'It's why I don't feel guilty about being in the FFFC. If I don't care, nobody can hurt me again.'

Agnes opened her mouth, but nothing came out. She was excellent at hiding the anger at her father's death, and – apart from a few fleeting moments – Bettina excelled at bottling her fear. What were the other FFFC members hiding?

'Get out of here.' Bettina tapped her watch. 'You're going to be late for work.'

Agnes sped off, as Bettina's bitter voice followed her up the corridor. 'Average at best. The nerve of him. Jahmar wasn't worth the points.'

Chapter Sixteen

All day long the conversation with Bettina replayed itself. The dance teacher had her very specific reasons for being in the FFFC, but what about Agnes? Why did she feel the need to score points by deceiving others? She could surely have a laugh with her friends without needing to play such a toxic game. Maybe it was time to call it a day. Today's shift seemed never-ending. It was day nine of sixteen and her very bones ached with tiredness. She needed an early night but had promised to meet Tony. It wouldn't take that long to look at some drawings. He'd have only done one or two at most today. Yes, a quick catch-up and then bed.

Luckily, her two sick colleagues had returned to work, and it enabled Agnes to exit the galley bang on time. But she wasn't going straight to the deck. She might be exhausted but that didn't mean she wanted to turn up smelling like yesterday's takeaway remains. A quick shower would also work wonders. She caught her foot, tripped into the cabin and almost face-planted the desk. Righting herself, she saw a note.

I'm on a date! I'll reveal all later. Mx

Very interesting. She kicked off her shoes and was midway through unbuttoning her chef whites when there was a knock. Had the date gone so horribly wrong, Maria was unable to open the door? But it was Tony with bloodshot eyes, looking ten times worse than this morning.

'I followed you,' he said with no trace of remorse.

Agnes grabbed hold of his jumper, dragged him inside and slammed the door. 'What are you doing here? I could get into serious trouble. Guests aren't supposed to be in staff quarters.'

'I didn't know where else to go.' He slumped into a fold-down chair. 'I can't find Patrick and I can't talk to Jahmar about this.'

'What's wrong, what's happened?' Had somebody died? Agnes mentally slapped herself. Of course not. He wouldn't be coming to her with something like that, he'd go straight to Jahmar or his other friends. So why was he here?

'We had a terrible fight.'

'Who had a fight?'

'Me and my fiancée.'

'Why do you never use her name?' It seemed a logical question but, hunched over in his seat, Tony stared at her as if she had two heads. 'I don't know what she's called. You've never said her name. I think it's weird that's all.'

He giggled uncontrollably but it quickly descended into sobbing. 'You're right. It can't be normal not to mention your fiancée's name, can it.'

'So, what is her name?' Agnes prompted.

'Sashana, or Sasha for short.'

'Okay then, Sasha and you fought. Couples fight all the time. What's the big deal, what's so bad about this one?'

'That's just the thing. We don't fight, ever. Sasha tells me what to do and I do it.' His eyes flicked around the room and came to rest on a cupboard. Agnes stood up and extracted a bottle of vodka and two glasses. She poured a shot into his and then, why the hell not, poured herself one. 'You read my mind.'

'It wasn't that hard, to be fair,' she replied as they both knocked them back and he signalled for another. 'I hope you don't mind me saying this, but you sound like a doormat.'

He slugged back another and chuckled. 'That's exactly what I was … until I met you.'

'I think you need to stop drinking right now.' She screwed on the lid and placed the bottle back in the cupboard. When she turned, he had a peaceful expression.

'You're right. I need to explain this when I'm sober. So you understand it's me talking and not the drink.'

'Okay.' She perched on the opposite chair. It was undoubtably a bad idea to encourage him, but he needed a sounding board and why not her? It was sometimes good to talk to a stranger. 'Explain away.'

She listened as he ran through his relationship. To start with he was besotted, he worshipped the ground she walked on and couldn't believe it (and still didn't) when she agreed to go out with him. It was wonderful. They only had eyes for one another and didn't need anyone else. But then things started to subtly change. He'd say or do something to offend, and she'd sulk. He was quick to make amends and over the years he'd placated and adapted his behaviour to avoid arguments. But he wouldn't hear a word said against her. She was the best thing to happen to him. As a result, some friendships suffered, and his family became more and more reticent to visit. If she told him to jump, he said how high. Her dreams were now his. He worked and all his money went into their joint account. She ran the finances, and he had no idea how much anything cost, what their outgoings were, how much she contributed (if anything), but only that it never seemed to be enough. Any time spent as a couple was only ever in the company of her family or her friends.

'Good grief,' Agnes exclaimed. 'Do you have a backbone?'

'I know. I'm utterly pathetic,' he replied and swallowed hard. 'I know this is down to me. I know I could have spoken up at any time. But I took the easy option because I couldn't believe somebody as beautiful and clever as Sasha would look twice at the likes of me. And then go on to love me and want to spend our lives together.'

'Why do you always put yourself down?' Agnes snapped. He had so much going for him. Why couldn't he see it? 'There's no such thing as an easy option. You should know that.'

'Of course there isn't. I reasoned away her behaviour because I know this is difficult to believe but I'm not perfect either.' Agnes smirked at his self-deprecation and was rewarded with a wink. 'I now know I was building a virtual prison with me as the only inmate. But then I boarded this cruise liner.'

Agnes gripped onto the plastic moulded chair; he was staring right at her. The dull trundling wheels of a heavily laden trolley passed outside and provided an excuse for her to break eye contact. Glancing back, she was sure a ghost of a smirk played on his lips, needle sharp irritation pricked her skin. Why did he annoy her so much?

'Okay, so what are you trying to tell me? That you've been a spineless wimp for years but suddenly after nine days at sea you're this new man who stands up for himself?' Her tone was severe, but he didn't seem offended at all. If anything, the man seemed to be enjoying himself. 'It all sounds rather implausible don't you think? And I don't see what any of this has to do with me.'

And this time he broke into a cheeky grin. 'Are you usually this dense? Or just with guests?'

'I-I don't … I don't know what you're talking about.'

He arched an eyebrow and her stomach slowly flipped. 'I think you know exactly what I'm talking about, but if you want me to spell it out I will. You helped me see myself. You helped me to see the person I was, and I didn't like him. In fact, I loathed him.'

'That's a bit harsh, don't you think?' Her voice was quiet now. 'You've got lots of great qualities.'

That smile played again on his gorgeous lips and her heart rate kicked up a notch. 'Well, that's very nice of you to say so. And that's what you enabled me to do. That despite being an absolute arse, you saw enough in me to get me off that nightmare horse. And despite me ruining your lovely picture you handed me a set of pencils and a notepad and gave me gentle words of encouragement.'

Agnes shifted uncomfortably. He was laying far too much emphasis on everyday actions. 'But anyone would do that. I didn't do anything special.'

'Yes, you did.' He grabbed her hands and held on. 'Do you know when I told you somebody said I was rubbish at art and should get a proper job and stop wasting my time?' She nodded. 'Well, that person was Sasha.'

'No.' Agnes frowned and mentally chalked up another mark against the woman.

Tony nodded. 'And what you made me realise was she did it to sabotage me, because she had her own agenda. Sasha wants to keep me in a box, control me and carve out the life she wants for her. I despise my job. Every day another part of me dies and she knows that. But at least I have my girls to come home to.'

'Are you sure about this, Tony?' He was so certain, but doubts niggled at Agnes. The woman couldn't be all bad, surely. 'Are you not getting a bit carried away with the holiday vibe? Even if Sasha said you were no good, that was years ago. You said it yourself, it's why you went into IT. I bet she wouldn't think the same thing now. How could she, you're so good.'

'No,' he shouted and banged his hand on the table. 'Yesterday I discovered she'd swanned off on a three-day jolly with her mates and didn't think twice about leaving my three girls to fend for themselves.' His voice continued to rise, and Agnes didn't intervene. He needed to get this off his chest. 'She didn't give a shit about their welfare. She didn't deem it important enough to tell me. Or ask for my family's help because she can't abide them. And then she had the sheer nerve to finally return my call today and kick off at me for keeping secrets. She admitted to deliberately shutting them in the kitchen and said it served me right for daring to consider going to college.'

He was up now, pacing the cabin, yanking at his short wiry hair. 'Who does something like that? They didn't have any water left when my mum found them. What if I hadn't rung home? It makes me sick to even think about what she did. And I'm such an idiot I thought she'd be happy at me going to art school. But I was swiftly informed that she'd made sure I wouldn't be.'

Agnes wasn't sure if it was the vodka, the lack of sleep or the long hours but her brain couldn't keep up. 'How did Sasha know about art school? Did Jahmar tell her?'

'No, he kept quiet.' Tony leaned against the wall and closed his eyes. 'We've got a home computer and—'

'She read your emails.' How many people had become unstuck because they'd forgotten to log off?

He laughed bitterly. 'You'd think I'd be more security conscious, working in IT. She didn't just read them. Sasha contacted the college and said due to a family bereavement I was no longer seeking to enrol.'

'No way.' Agnes was upright, arms windmilling wildly. 'Ring them back, explain your fiancée is a witch. You have to get back in. You must. She can't have messed everything up, can she?'

'It's okay, I've got it all sorted.' He took her hands and kissed them gently. 'And do you know what made me realise how wrong everything was?'

Agnes gripped on to his hands; she didn't want to let go. 'What could be worse than everything you've told me?'

'I wanted to prove to her that I do have raw talent, so I showed her my sketch.'

'Well, she must have been impressed by that?' They were still holding hands, their faces centimetres from one another.

'She said it was piss poor and if I thought I had any talent I was unhinged.'

His arms were wrapped around her waist and hers were on his chest. 'I-I don't know what to say. She's wrong. You must listen to me, Tony. She's very wrong.'

'I love how you get so affronted on my behalf.' He reached back and carefully undid her clip and she shook out her long hair. 'It's alright, I know she's talking crap. I took your advice and went to Vlad. He said I'm rough around the edges, but I do have natural talent that needs developing. And that's what I'm going to do.'

She tilted her head back as he dropped delicious kisses down her neck. 'So, what happens now?'

'I have five full days left aboard and I intend to have a bloody good time.' His fingers pulled apart the press studs on her shirt and it fell to the floor. 'And then I'm going to go back home and break the news to Sasha that the wedding's off. Because getting married to that bitch would be the biggest mistake of my life.'

Agnes silently agreed as he unhooked her bra. 'Don't you think you should maybe tell her before you get back?'

'Agnes, if I do that, I'll not have a house to go back to. She'll probably change the locks and at the very least shred all my clothes.'

His hands were on her waistband and in a fluid motion he unzipped and then slid down her trousers. She levered off her shoes with each foot and then stepped out of her trousers. 'Do you think she'd do that?'

'Oh yes, without a shadow of a doubt. Thank God, Mum has my cats.' He gently kissed her lips. It was wonderful.

'I stink of deep-fat fryers,' she whispered as he kissed her neck.

'I don't care. Do you know how long I've wanted to run my fingers through your hair? How long I've wanted to kiss your lips? And how long I've wanted to—'

'No, we can't.' Agnes stepped back.

'But why not?' He sounded hurt. 'I'm not getting married anymore.'

'Because I'm not the answer.'

'What do you mean?'

'You're replacing Sasha with me. I'm not the love of your life. I'm a young woman you've met on a cruise ship and in six days' time we'll part ways.'

'Why are you being like this?'

He was still fully clothed, and she was semi-naked but made no move to get dressed. 'Because I need you to understand that this is going nowhere.'

'Don't you want this?' He was leaning against her work rota, frowning. She could understand why he was confused. And so was she. Here was the perfect chance to earn FFFC points and she was throwing them away.

'That's not the point.'

'That's the whole point, surely? I don't understand why there's a problem?'

'The problem is I don't want to be emotionally invested in …' Agnes pointed to the pair of them. 'In whatever you want to call this.'

'But we *are* emotionally invested. Unless you sleep with men you don't care about? Is that what you're trying to tell me?'

The FFFC league table flashed up before her, but she blotted it out. 'Of course I don't. I'm just trying to explain that we aren't going to fall in love and live happily ever after.'

He laughed. 'I didn't think for one minute that we were.'

Agnes shook her head. 'I disagree. I think you're placing a great deal of importance on us. I think you've realised how many years of your life you've wasted with Sasha, and you want to make up for lost time. You believe I'm going to take her place. But I'm telling you now that's not going to happen. I have big plans that I won't change for anyone. I'm going to be a Head Chef on a cruise ship in the next three years and nothing is going to stand in my way.'

'I've said it before and I'll say it again, you are unbelievably direct. But two can play at that game.' He stripped off his jumper and T-shirt and slapped his sixpack. 'You stand there and tell me to my face that you don't want this, and I'll walk out of this cabin, never to bother you again.'

Chapter Seventeen

Agnes never thought you could die of embarrassment but in that second, she came close. Out of her mouth came a low-pitched guttural sound. A primeval groan of unsuppressed longing and desire. A mating call. They silently stared at one another but this time when good-natured catcalling broke out in the corridor, she maintained eye contact.

'Based on past feedback, I'd like to think I'm a good lover,' Tony said. 'But never in my relatively short existence has a female made that sound in my company when I'm across the room from her.'

She stood rooted to the spot as he prised off his shoes and removed his trousers. They were both in their underwear. And then he dropped his boxer shorts. Oh my. But still, she held her ground.

'I need to hear you say that you know this is going nowhere after this cruise comes to an end.'

He held up one hand and placed another on an imaginary bible. 'I promise that I will allow Agnes Karapetsa to abuse my body in any way she sees fit for the duration of this cruise. And then cast me aside like a plate of food that has failed to reach her exacting standards.'

She stood with hands on her hips, scowling. A half-naked woman bristling with anger. She knew she must look ridiculous. 'Tony! Say it!'

He stroked his chin. 'This has to be the strangest seduction ever, don't you think?'

'There won't be any seduction taking place at the rate you're going.' She glowered at him but all he did was grin. 'I'm going to count to three. There will not be a four.'

He laughed out loud. 'That's what my mum used to say to us when we misbehaved.'

'One.'

He walked purposefully towards her. 'I know you want me.'

'Two.'

He ran his fingers down her spine, until they hooked underneath her knicker elastic.

She narrowed her eyes. 'Two and a half.'

'My God, you're beautiful.'

'Thr—'

'Okay, okay,' he whispered in her ear. 'I know we are going nowhere after this cruise comes to an end.'

She slipped off her underwear. 'See that wasn't too difficult, was it?'

'I didn't want you to think I was a pushover,' he joked as his eyes hungrily devoured her body. 'Let's make the next five days count.'

She couldn't have put it better herself.

Chapter Eighteen

Day twelve and it was after midnight when Agnes crept back to her cabin. Unsurprisingly, Maria's bed was empty. Love (or more likely lust) was certainly in the air. She peeled off her shift dress. It had barely been worth putting it on. After work, she'd quickly scurried back to her cell and stayed just long enough to change, before racing up to the top deck for a second evening with Tony.

The first time in her cabin had been intense, glorious revenge sex up against the cupboard with the contents rattling and clanking. Tony had funnelled all his anger and rage at his fiancée, and Agnes revelled in it, calling Sasha a spoilt, selfish princess who deserved the betrayal. A bitch who'd brought everything on herself. And he'd joined in, swearing, and cursing his ex-lover's name. The chance of Maria walking in heightened the thrill but in no time at all it was over, and he was gone. Agnes didn't feel guilty.

She felt alive.

And tonight, a quickie up against the cold metal hulk of the ship as it powered through the darkness. He'd yanked up her dress, dropped his shorts and as people's voices drifted towards them, they'd fed off the excitement of getting caught. But this time his anger was gone, and they didn't mention Sasha's name. It hadn't ended there though; they'd snuck inside the deserted dance studio. She'd flicked on spotlights, and they'd danced between the shadows, their bodies entwined, only separating to undress, one tantalising item at a time, until they were skin to skin. And this time they'd made love, slowly savouring each other. Afterwards they'd retrieved their clothes strewn across the parquet floor. Switching off the lights, Agnes was satisfied they'd left the room as they found it but did wonder if somebody was going to find clammy handprints on the bank of mirrors tomorrow morning.

She shut off the shower, quickly towelling dry before studying her reflection. Her eyes shone; her skin glowed but she chewed her lower lip. In twenty-four hours, they'd gone from a quick shag to making love. Tony had been right; they were emotionally involved with one another. He'd solemnly promised a no-strings-attached affair, ending when he walked down the gangway and headed home. But Agnes wasn't so sure, and her doubts niggled away. She had an awful feeling he wanted more than she was prepared to give.

She exhaled slowly because it wasn't just him. She'd always been ambitious. Even as a kid she'd hated losing. She always wanted to be the best at whatever she put her mind to. Otherwise, what was the point? People who said it was the taking part that mattered were kidding nobody. And once she had an inkling Tony wanted more than artistic tips from her, she'd envisaged storming up the FFFC league table, amassing the points with her sexual shenanigans and smugly grinning as she lifted the trophy aloft.

But when it came to it, she couldn't. Scoring points off Tony didn't sit right with her. He already had one manipulative female in his life. She didn't want to be a second. And that spoke volumes. Maybe she was going soft? Her previous on-board dalliances had been purely physical. She hadn't exactly jumped into the sack with countless passengers, but she wasn't an angel either. However, her connection with Tony went beyond the usual superficial chit-chat and a holiday shag; he was the only one she'd cared about.

She nodded at her reflection, standing there in cartoon sheep pyjamas. Get a grip, Karapetsa. Stop over-analysing everything and have some fun. You deserve it.

Pep talk completed and time for bed. She didn't need to bother switching on the cabin light as it was only a few steps to her bunk, so in pitch darkness she hauled herself upwards.

Fingers brushed her hand and a soft voice whispered. 'Hello, stranger.'

Agnes screamed, shot backwards, collided with the table, and landed in a crumpled heap on the floor.

'Are you trying to give me a heart attack?'

The bunk light snapped on and a pair of huge brown eyes peered down. 'Been having fun, have we?'

'Not as much as you, I reckon.' Agnes clambered to her feet, rubbing her left elbow.

Maria extracted herself from beneath the duvet, dropped onto the floor and grabbed two glasses and a bottle of coffee liqueur from the cupboard.

'Come on, spill the beans.' Maria grinned. 'Tell me every single debauched detail. And don't feed me any crap about requiring beauty sleep because you're humming with post-sex satisfaction.'

Agnes necked her drink and poured another. 'No deal. I want to know about this mysterious date. You left a note two days ago and I haven't seen you since, so I'm assuming it went well.'

It had gone infinitely better than that. The flirtatious photographer and her former schoolmate were sweet on one another. This wasn't simply a roll in the sack, it was the real deal and the pair had post-cruise-ship plans.

Agnes sat on the edge of her seat, waving an empty glass in the air. 'Are you serious? Would you honestly give all this up for some bloke? You've always told me how much you love this lifestyle, getting to photograph some amazing places. Even if it means putting up with awkward punters. Won't you be bored stuck in one place?'

Maria's face beamed; she'd never looked happier. 'But that's the beauty of our plan, we're going to travel and see the world. We're going where we want to go. No more cramped cabins, no need to tolerate ludicrous guest demands through gritted teeth. We'll be on the open road, taking life as it comes, and I can't wait.'

Her friend bounced up and down on her seat, excitedly explaining how travel photography was big business and with a website-savvy boyfriend they would work remotely. Agnes happily listened to all Maria's plans. What a shame, there'd be no time to discuss Tony before bed. She gave a dramatic yawn and announced it was getting late, but she wasn't going to get away that easily.

Maria's hand shot out and grabbed Agnes's wrist. 'Not so fast, mademoiselle. I've heard reports of a certain groom-to-be being seen in the company of a future Head Chef.'

'It's complicated.' Agnes chewed her fingernail.

'Are you shagging him or not?'

'It's not like that,' Agnes protested. But her loved-up friend was having none of it.

'Are you, or are you not, having sex with Monsieur Acebi?'

'Yes, but—'

'But nothing.' Maria slammed the table with both hands and laughed. 'Well, you certainly had me fooled with your holier-than-thou preachings on the sanctity of marriage. You could give Rodriguez a run for his money.' And what could Agnes say? Nobody knew Tony had called off the engagement, so she sat there burning with shame and indignation as Maria probed. 'Is he any good? How many times? Do you feel guilty?' A pause and then, 'It doesn't bother me. If you're fine with it, that's all that matters.'

Agnes sunk lower and lower into the chair, glumly staring at her empty glass. The coffee liqueur sat heavily in her stomach and all she wanted to do was hide under the covers. 'I need to go to bed.'

Maria sprung up. 'I'm not surprised, after all your antics. You must be knackered. You do know what this means don't you?'

'No, what does it mean?' Agnes replied flatly and tugged at her cotton pyjamas.

'That you could win the league. Play your cards right and you might be the first of us to break up a wedding. Fancy that.'

'No, I'm not—'

Maria necked back her remaining drink. 'Sorry, sweetie. I must dash, a gorgeous man is keeping the bed warm for me.'

And before Agnes had the chance to explain that she wasn't submitting any points, the cabin door slammed shut. She was left alone, uneasy at the disapproving eyes staring down from all the photos. Even her faithful teddy bear was facing the wall.

Chapter Nineteen

It was surprisingly still at the top of Mount Srd. No wind, a clear blue sky and down below the UNESCO walled city of Dubrovnik in all her glory.

The morning's tour had lived up to all expectations. But this time it wasn't Jahmar who'd triumphed. It was Patrick. The snapshot into 1,400 years of history, followed by a two-hour off-road safari had been his advanced wedding gift. Jahmar had insisted on paying for everybody else. And that stuck in Tony's throat. He wasn't getting married but apart from Agnes nobody else knew. He kept up the groom-to-be facade for everyone and the happiness wasn't feigned. Agnes, he rolled the name around on his tongue. A sweet sound, a red-hot sexy sound and he couldn't wait for more. What had it been, two days since they'd given in to temptation? Early in the morning and late at night they met for a tantalisingly short snippet of time.

Oh, but how they made the most of those fleeting moments. Time accelerated when they were together but dragged while apart. How could this just be a holiday romance? He couldn't understand her refusal to accept anything more. They were meant to be together. He'd never felt this way, even about Sasha. He was her indentured servant, pathetically grateful for the attentions of a beautiful but cruel mistress. But with Agnes, they were equals. He'd make her see that there was a future together for them. How could there not be?

Sure, she wanted to be a top chef but wasn't London an ideal place to make her mark? He'd yet to mention it, fearful of her response, because there were still many similarities between his ex and his current lover. Both were strong, confident women who brokered no arguments if they believed they were right. Agnes was remarkably direct. No doubt about that. She spoke her mind and tough if you didn't agree. But then she was kind-hearted, naturally talented, and encouraged his dreams. She'd gained her position on this ship through her own hard work. Where would he be without her? Easy. About to marry a woman who'd never worked hard for a thing in her life. A woman who he firmly believed didn't love or certainly didn't respect him. Two days since their huge fight and he'd heard nothing more from her. And for once he wasn't going to be the first to fold. No way. Every time he thought of Thunder, Penny and Doc his blood boiled. But at least they were now safe with his mum and each day he'd called home to coo over them.

Only four days before he flew back home. He wasn't entirely sure how to break the news. It was his house so by rights Sasha should move out. But he didn't expect it to be that straightforward. Perhaps Sasha herself wanted out but the lure of a big white wedding was too much of a temptation. There was no point stressing about the inevitable repercussions. He'd think about it on the flight home.

'Fantastic view, don't you think?'

It was Jahmar. They might have sorted out their Agnes quarrel and were back to normal, but for how long? Tony was going to have to accept he'd lose the friendship, along with his fiancée.

'Absolutely awesome. Thanks again for the cruise. It's been brilliant.'

'It's my pleasure.' Jahmar adjusted the cuffs of his silk shirt. 'Better to enjoy your money than have it languishing in a tax-free haven.'

'Well, I wouldn't know about that.' And again, that ripple of guilt. He was going to have to do some serious overtime to pay back the stag-do cruise. But then again if he wasn't fixing all of Sasha's mates' computers, he'd have bags of time.

'I caught up with Sasha last night,' Jahmar said in a light and chatty tone.

'That's nice.' Tony stared at the cruise ship. From this distance it was toy-sized, and he wondered what Agnes was doing.

'She said you'd had a fight and had yet to apologise.'

'Fancy that.' He looked down on the city walls and wondered how many lovers had walked hand in hand, declaring undying love, only to have it crumble to dust.

'Look it isn't my place—'

'No, it's not.' His voice was firm, and Jahmar raised an eyebrow.

'I just want what's best for my sister and my best mate. That's all.'

Visions of Sasha and Agnes played on a loop. Two lovers, two strong women, two alternate futures. But only one brought Tony joy. 'So do I.' And he meant it. Sasha needed somebody else, somebody who'd tolerate or stand up to all the crap she dished out. But that wasn't going to be him anymore, he'd paid his dues.

'If she loves you, she'll forgive you.' Jahmar winked. 'Love always finds a way.'

The comment hung in the air and Tony reappraised his best mate. The glint in the eye was back, along with the swagger and that confident smile that always melted women's hearts.

'You've met somebody else, haven't you?'

But this time the playboy wasn't smug. He didn't boast or brag, but instead, there was a shy smile. 'I might have. It's too early to say. But … well, maybe you'll meet her soon.'

'Oh my God,' Tony declared and took an overdramatic step backwards. 'I do believe the man has finally fallen in love. Can that be possible?'

Jahmar placed an arm around Tony's shoulders. 'Time will tell. Anyway, it looks as if somebody else wants a word.'

Patrick stood on the clifftop, staring intently at the cruise ship.

'Is everything okay?' Tony asked.

His older friend stretched and then smiled. He looked different somehow. It was subtle and probably nobody else would have noticed. But Tony saw it around the eyes. A smoothing out of the lines. A contented face. 'Are you enjoying the cruise?' His eyes flicked to where Jahmar was regaling their mates with some amusing anecdote about twins, Monaco and a high-speed car chase. It sounded implausible but you never knew. After all, how many people had Lewis Hamilton on speed dial? 'I know not everyone in my circle of friends is your cup of tea.'

Patrick laughed. It was a throaty, big-hearted, I-smoke-too-much-of-what-I-shouldn't sound. 'As long as you're happy, son. That's all I care about. I can tolerate any amount of bollocks for that.' His eyes scrutinised Tony as if he was seeing him after a long absence. 'And you are, aren't you? Over the last few days, you've come alive. It's as if a light is shining out, that joyous optimism you had as a kid. It's been absent for quite some time. I can honestly say, I haven't seen you this happy since Tottenham won the league cup.'

'Are you mellowing out on me, old man?' Tony teased but it was another sign that him and Agnes should be together. She was the reason he practically skipped along, instead of dragging his feet.

'Maybe, but seriously I'm with Jahmar on this, we both want the best for you.' Patrick cast another look down the mountain to the distant harbour. 'And as an "old man," I'm telling you, embrace the best of everything because life is too short to squander.'

'And are you content, Father Time?' Tony replied and joined Patrick in staring at the floating hotel. Its white hull shone out like a guiding star. But guiding him to what end? 'I've also seen a change in you since this cruise. I do believe you're having the time of your life.'

'And you'd be right there, young 'un. I do believe this cruise has been the making of both of us.'

Chapter Twenty

Agnes exited the kitchen and was rushing back to her cabin for a quick change when Bettina slipped a note into her hand, winked and walked off.

Go to the Grand Staircase. Do not go to your cabin. The clock is ticking.

She curiously made her way to the twin curved steps. A real 'Cinderella misplaced her glass slipper' backdrop. And there he was. The breath caught in her throat. He stood at the very top in a tux, holding a single red rose. Her eyes tracked his every movement as he descended, and they were finally face to face.

'For you, gracious lady.' He held out the flower.

'James Bond, eat your heart out,' she whispered, fearful of breaking the spell. People brushed passed them, but she barely registered them. 'You look amazing.'

He kissed her on the nose. 'So do you.'

'I'm still in my work clothes. I look a state.'

'Never fear, fair maiden. Follow me.'

He took her hand and they walked into one of the swishest boutiques. And there behind the counter was Maria, grinning from ear to ear.

'Welcome, mademoiselle. I understand you're in the market for a gorgeous gown this evening?'

'I … I—'

Maria brushed the protests aside. 'Come through to the changing rooms and I'll show you what we have.' Agnes handed Tony the rose and followed her friend into a cubicle. 'They're on loan for one night only. Drop them back off first thing tomorrow morning and for God's sake don't damage them.'

Agnes caressed the floor-length strapless dress. It was a deep magenta taffeta-and-sequined creation. Truly stunning. And nestled inside tissue paper was an exquisite pair of strappy stiletto sandals. Gobsmacked, she could only stand and stare. Things like this didn't happen in real life, or not to her anyway. 'Well, what are you waiting for?' Maria admonished. 'The clock is ticking, get a move on.' But she gave a wink and closed the cubicle door.

'Wow!' two voices declared in unison.

Agnes spun around in her heels. 'I feel like a princess.'

'No, you're a queen,' Tony said firmly. 'My queen for the night.'

Maria shooed them out of the boutique. 'Enjoy. And Agnes, there'll be a clean uniform for you in the changing room tomorrow morning.'

He took her arm and they proceeded, like a regal couple on the way to a glittering ball. And this time, Agnes took in the admiring glances from those they swept past. It gave her a thrill to see other contented couples smile at them and then at one another, or the wistful glances of those who were seeking that special someone. But she was puzzled. They were drawing a great deal of attention. Hardly the behaviour of a loving fiancé.

'Aren't you worried Jahmar or your other friends will see us?' They were still on the upper decks; the dinner sittings were over and plenty of people milled about.

He smiled enigmatically and patted her arm. 'Don't worry about it. Jahmar is in love, whereabouts unknown. Undoubtedly he will only have eyes for the unknown lady in question. Patrick excused himself after we returned from our day trip saying he didn't feel well and wanted a lie down. And the rest of the lads are tied up in some marathon James Bond movie fest. So we're perfectly safe.'

They were now gliding along the deck that housed the top-tier accommodation. Tony tapped the key card against a cabin door that put hers to shame. They stepped inside and she sank into the deep carpet. Words failed her. It was better than the photos.

'You can close your mouth now,' he teased. 'You resemble a fish from the aquarium downstairs.'

She grabbed his arm to steady herself. 'Holy shit, how the hell did you pull this off?'

They were inside one of the penthouse suites. Once, on a whim, she'd gone online to check out how much it cost to stay in one of them and nearly had a fit. There was no expense spared here. The downstairs was at least ten times the size of her cabin with wrap-around sofas. A wall of glass led out onto a huge balcony with a hot tub. A mouth-watering aroma of spices, fish and steak filled her nostrils. It came from the enormous dining table laden with a three-course meal. She jumped as Tony popped the cork of a very expensive-looking bottle of champagne. He handed her a glass and the delicious bubbles slid down far too easily. This was a lifestyle she could get used to.

'Come on, follow me.' He held out his hand and they ascended the spiral staircase to the upper level. A massive bed with an inordinate number of pillows and cushions took centre stage. The bathroom had all sorts of delicious, scented lotions and potions and she caught sight of herself in the mirror. The little girl from northern Greece playing make-believe with her Prince Charming. He wrapped his arms around her waist. 'Do you like it?'

'Do I like it? I love it. But you still haven't answered my question. How did you manage all this?'

He raised an eyebrow. 'That's my little secret. But enough talk, let's eat.' The food was amazing, and they devoured everything. Tony raised his glass. 'To what comes next.'

'To what comes next,' she replied and grinned. 'And speaking of which, do you fancy a bit of skinny-dipping?'

The dress and tuxedo were laid gently on the sofa and, shivering slightly, Agnes slid back the balcony door and slipped into the warm water. The moonlit ocean shimmered as Tony pulled her naked body against his, kissed her mouth and neck and she laughed with sheer joy. The night passed like a dream. Was this her life? They made love in the enormous bed, slept in each other's arms, woke, made love, slept, woke and made love again.

The sun crept over the horizon and the crashing realisation hit. She needed to go to work. Dressing quickly, she breathed a massive sigh of relief. The dress was still perfect. Not a mark on it. Hand in hand, they quietly closed the door and raced back to the boutique. As promised, her clean uniform was there, and she quickly changed. Reality sucked.

They stood in the glass-domed atrium, the clouds overhead casting shadows across his sad face. She brushed a finger against his stubble. He took her hand and kissed it. 'I wish you didn't have to go to work. I wish we could spend all day together.'

'So do I.' She sighed and they reluctantly descended the stairs. Their footsteps slowed, to delay the inevitable. Agnes had deliberately gone out of her way but finally, they could put it off no longer.

In the foyer there were various double doors leading to guest accommodation. Usually, the doors stood open with a constant flow of traffic but this early in the morning, they were shut. 'This is my floor.' He nodded towards one of the doors. 'I best sneak back.'

After one last embrace, the door opened on its own accord and another amorous couple spilled out.

Chapter Twenty-One

For a split second, Agnes wasn't sure who was more surprised.

'Oh, hello there,' she managed in a light-hearted manner. 'This is the first time I've seen you anything other than immaculately turned out.'

'Good morning.' Sebastian attempted to smooth out his wrinkled shirt while grinning from ear to ear.

Agnes watched Tony's face register utter confusion. 'What the—?'

'Oh, shit,' Patrick spluttered, stepped back and slammed the door shut.

'I-I had no idea.' Tony stared at Sebastian and then Agnes, before wrenching the door open and likewise disappearing.

Agnes tightened her ponytail for something to do. 'I guess I now know who's been putting a smile on your face.'

'He does.' Sebastian gave a shy smile and adjusted his metal-rimmed spectacles. 'I'm sorry to do this to you, but I think I need to go after them.'

And in less than three seconds, she was alone. There was nothing she could do and besides she wasn't entirely sure what the state of play was anyway. Did Tony not know Patrick was gay? Or was it that he just didn't know about Sebastian? From the various comments dropped about Patrick being a ladies' man, she suspected it was the former. Oh well, she was sure it'd all work out. The relentless hum of the engines continued. Soon the ship's residents would all be up and readying themselves for another day.

Today's port of call was Corfu Town, and they'd remain docked until late afternoon. Some passengers made it no further than the old town, strolling around its impressive walls and admiring the Venetian architecture. Others ventured a little further, always with one eye on the clock in fear of returning too late. And then there was Tony and his friends who intended to cram as much in as possible. They had an island tour booked which took in a hilltop café used as a location in the James Bond film *For Your Eyes Only* and then they were going paragliding. The fact Tony was terrified of heights was neither here nor there and Agnes remained quiet on the whole torturous nature of UK stag-do etiquette. However, it meant Tony would have little time to quiz Patrick this morning. She'd find out about it tonight. Last night had been truly magical, and it would get her through the day. With a light step, she set off, merrily humming away and was so engrossed in her own happy thoughts that she barely registered a moody Rodriguez stalking up the corridor. At the last minute, she called out a chirpy hello. He stopped dead and scowled so hard that the gap between his perfectly shaped eyebrows vanished.

'Good God. Am I the only person not getting laid around here,' he huffed.

The tune died on her lips. 'What? I'm just—'

'Basking in the afterglow of sex,' he groused further while realising that a shirt button had popped off to reveal his sizeable and unusually hairy tummy. It did little to improve his mood. 'Don't bother to deny it, girl. You're making me sick with your smugness.'

He stormed past, muttering all the way down the corridor. Was it that obvious, Agnes wondered, and tried but failed to stop smirking.

Chapter Twenty-Two

Corfu had long since vanished and Agnes shivered as a cool sea breeze whipped along the deck. She tightened the scarf around her neck and dug her hands further into fleece-lined pockets. Where was Tony? She had no idea of his cabin number and wouldn't have gone anyway because of Jahmar. She didn't even know his mobile and had never thought to ask him for it. So she continued to wait. The cold leeched into her bones and she was on the verge of leaving when Sebastian appeared. He was out of breath and sent profuse apologies from Tony who was with Patrick.

'Is everything okay?' Agnes straightened. Had she been too quick to think everything would be fine? Sebastian nodded emphatically. There was nothing to worry about, but Tony wanted to spend time getting to know the real Patrick.

'They've asked me to join them,' Sebastian explained. Agnes heard the hope and longing in her friend's soft-spoken voice, and any annoyance with Tony vanished.

She reached out and grasped his hand. 'I'm happy for you.'

He came and sat beside her, and they linked arms. 'I have a good feeling about this. I think … no, I know he's the one.'

They sat in comfortable silence and stared out towards the horizon where a dark sea met a shade lighter sky. After a few minutes, Agnes unlinked her arm. 'Go and enjoy yourself. Don't waste any more time sitting here with me.'

And even though it was still cold, she remained on deck and closed her eyes. She listened to the wind catching at canvas deckchairs to her left. She listened to murmurings and snatches of laughter that carried through the air. Her lungs filled with fresh sea air but instead of being invigorated, she was struck with overwhelming loneliness. There was a sense of being a tiny insignificant speck floating on a huge body of water. At this exact moment, thousands of lives played out on board. How many of those were deliriously happy like Sebastian and Maria? How many were seeking new adventures like Tony and Patrick? And how many were wrapped up in playing a game like Bettina and Rodriguez? And what about her? What was she trying to achieve?

She stood up abruptly. She'd never been one to wallow in self-pity. It was time for bed. But first, she'd check her mobile for messages. She hadn't switched it on since yesterday and was curious about any changes to FFFC rankings. Her phone buzzed the latest results, but that couldn't be right. She switched it off and back on, believing there'd been some sort of glitch. But no, it was the same result. And what was worse, there was a string of comments congratulating her. She was now at the top of the leaderboard. But far from basking in glory, a rage was building. She deliberately hadn't input any scores, not wanting to profit from her relationship with Tony.

She paused, unwilling at first to admit it. She cared about him more today than she had yesterday and would care more about him tomorrow. He wasn't the one, but he wasn't there to be used and abused in a sordid game. The anger rose, like molten lava pushing upwards, ready to violently erupt and devour anything in its path. She had a good idea who'd done it, remembering Rodriguez's earlier comments. Why the hell was he butting in? To get his own back on Maria and Bettina no doubt. They'd stood their ground against him, and it had cost him the lead, so in revenge he'd knocked the two women off first and second position. The power of the score master to spread mayhem. Sebastian would never have done such a thing. Her hands were shaking as she held the phone. Rodriguez input the scores, there was no other explanation for it. Well, she was going to have it out with him.

In less than ten minutes, she was outside his cabin braying on the door and demanding entrance. She knew he was in there because of the tray of dirty plates stacked in the corridor.

Rodriguez took all his meals in his cabin. Rumour had it that this was so nobody knew exactly how much he ate.

The door was thrown open and there he stood in a neon pink terry towelling bathrobe, enormous penguin slippers and a head full of rollers topped with a hairnet. She would have burst out laughing if she wasn't so furious.

'This had better be good,' he thundered. 'I'm watching reruns of *Little House on the Prairie.*'

She barged into the cabin, slamming the door behind her, and stuck the league table under his nose. 'Are you responsible for this?'

He glanced at the screen. 'As I have been forced into the degrading position of last place, I have no other option but to input all the scores I'm sent. Heaven knows why I initially volunteered for the job.'

'But I didn't send you any scores.' She was practically screaming in his face.

'Don't be so ridiculous, girl. I never make mistakes.' He stormed across to his laptop and furiously typed away before scrolling through his mobile. Agnes watched as he flicked between the two. After several minutes he turned around. 'I'm most dreadfully sorry, my dear. You're quite right, I did receive scores, but they weren't from you.' He plonked himself down on a spindly wooden chair which creaked ominously. 'I'm not aware of this ever having happened before. A competitor deliberately submits fake results in the name of another competitor. This has serious consequences.'

Agnes coughed. 'The results aren't fake.'

'I mean, we don't even have a rule for this.'

'The results are true,' Agnes raised her voice.

He was inflating like one of the astronomically priced helium balloons they sold on board, because where else were you going to go to get one? 'Hold on a minute? You almost broke down my door, screaming like a banshee. And now you tell me the results are valid. You had better start explaining fast, because you're two seconds away from being hurled out of here.'

She crumpled into a tub chair. 'I like him. I didn't want to … but I do. And I didn't … so I didn't want to enter any points. He's worth more than a stupid game.'

He handed her a handkerchief. 'Oh dear, I see what you mean.'

She dried her eyes and blew her nose. Why could she not control her emotions? This was so embarrassing. She looked up and was surprised to find Rodriguez watching her with what could only be described as fatherly concern. To change the subject, she studied his cabin.

'Oh my, you've got a window.' She peered out into the darkness. There was nothing but churning water and a pitch-black sky.

It was her dream to have a cabin with natural light, and she wasn't alone. Staff talked in hushed tones about their longing for the far-off dream. They'd nod to one another and whisper reverently about waking up and knowing what time of the day it was without looking at your watch. And to have the option to see the sunrise or sunset from somewhere other than the staff deck. But then someone would laugh and say, when did they ever get the chance to enjoy either of those anyway? Agnes had confided in Tony that if she ever wavered slightly in her relentless desire to be a Head Chef, the dream of a cabin with a window drove her on.

'I've got one of the largest windows,' Rodriguez proudly boasted. 'Of course, the captain and his officers have the very best but I'm not far behind. The Director of Entertainment only has a miniscule porthole. He was supposed to have this cabin until I blew a gasket and doesn't he hate me for that.'

Agnes was also sure Rodriguez would rub that fact in at every given opportunity. He was protected on high; nobody could touch the man who could make the ferocious captain roar with laughter. And because of that, Rodriguez not only had a window but the luxury of a separate bedroom, and she was willing to bet her annual salary that he enjoyed spending time in his ensuite. The living area was understated chic with stylish furniture and an eclectic mix of worldwide artefacts and artwork. He had excellent taste, which she was surprised at. She'd expected his domain to be a monument to excess, but the only homage to ego was a wall of fame featuring black and white signed photos of him with the rich and famous.

She stood up and peered intently at them. 'You've met Sean Connery? Tony would be so jealous. He's obsessed with James Bond.'

Rodriguez came over to join her and straightened one of the frames that was a millimetre out. 'I've also met Roger Moore, Timothy Dalton and Pierce Brosnan. They were all the epitome of sophistication and extremely polite. I've also been in the same room as Daniel Craig, not long after they'd announced he was going to be the next James Bond. But I-I didn't have the guts to go up to him.'

'You were scared?' Agnes blurted out. 'I wouldn't think that was possible.'

'I am human, you know.' He sounded hurt and she realised maybe he wasn't all bluster after all. 'Getting back to the league table, I'm sorry but if the points are genuine, I cannot remove them. You do understand that don't you?' She nodded mutely and sat back down. A yawning gap opened inside her and she was crying again. He patted her shoulder. 'It's not nice when you fall for them is it?'

She dropped her head down. 'I don't want to play anymore.'

He moved away and she heard the tinkle of ice and liquid being poured into glasses. The next minute, something was placed between her hands. 'Drink that. It'll make you feel better.'

She took a sip of the deep purple concoction and hungrily liked her lips. 'Wow, this is wonderful.' It was swiftly followed by her stomach sending up such a howl of hunger that she clamped her hand over it to deaden the sound. 'I haven't had time to eat much today.'

From the well-stocked bar, he picked up a wall mounted handset. 'Darling it's me … yes, I know it's late, but this is a dire emergency. I have a delightful member of the galley crew here, who one day is going to be an outstanding Head Chef. Yes, Agnes Karapetsa, that's the one.' He gave her a wink as she blushed furiously. 'The thing is the poor love is absolutely famished after feeding the legions. Yes, I know pigs to the trough does spring to mind. As if we'd ever run out of food. Anyway, I know you'll be able to spring to her aid.' There was a pause as Rodriguez fiddled with his hairnet. 'Yes, yes that would be perfect, sweetie. You're a diamond, Louis. We'll expect him in the next few minutes. Ciao.'

'You've got your own line to Monsieur Baffier?' Agnes whispered, awestruck. 'The man's a three-Michelin-star chef. He's a god.' She'd never spoken to the man except to say 'yes, chef' and 'no, chef'. He could whip up incredible dishes and would not tolerate even the slightest drop in absolute perfection from his team. Many had thrown in the towel – or more accurately had the towel thrown at their head and then screamed at to get out of his kitchen. Only the best of the best survived. Agnes drank in his genius; he was her idol and the benchmark to hit.

'And he knows who you are, as well.' Rodriguez smiled. 'I've got a hotline to anywhere on this ship, my child. Is there anyone you'd like to ring? Maybe this Tony?' She shook her head. 'Would you perhaps like more suitable attire?' He gave a withering look at her ensemble. 'A bobble hat? Really, are you six? And why in God's name are you wearing corduroy trousers? They are for fussy, ancient male professors who only ever purchase clothes from thrift shops. Or spinsters who have given up on ever having a sexual encounter in their lives.'

'They're comfy and keep me warm,' Agnes grumbled. And she'd always thought she looked quite cute in her handknitted pompom hat.

'Darling.' Rodriguez adjusted his rollers. 'You owe it to yourself and others to always look glorious. Just because you spend most of your days in chef whites does not give you the right to go about in your spare time dressed like a bag lady. Fashion isn't about comfort, you know.'

Agnes narrowed her eyes. 'I haven't seen many catwalk models parading down the runway with Pingu attached to their toes.'

He sighed in the manner of an exasperated teacher whose dim student can't comprehend simple addition. 'Obviously, it's their job to stalk around the place in divine stilettos as a lesson to us all.' He winked and tapped his nose. 'But I'm telling you, behind the scenes it's a catfight to get their tiny mittens on oversized animals slippers. Bless the poor things, they don't have an ounce of fat between them, so need all the warmth they can get.'

Agnes laughed, and ten minutes later she was in matching footwear and a dressing gown and chomping down on a mouth-watering gourmet pizza. It was like having her own private stand-up show as he rattled off joke after joke and funny stories drawn from life afloat. She was snorting with laughter and thoroughly enjoying herself.

'Thank you for cheering me up.' She dried her eyes. 'I'm having such a good time.'

'It's my pleasure. I enjoy making people laugh.'

After a few drinks, Agnes plucked up the courage to ask questions she'd always been too scared to mention before. 'What's the deal with you and Sebastian? Why do you hate each other so much?'

He shook his head. 'Not so fast. There needs to be a trade.' She gulped nervously. What did he want in return? 'You need to dish the dirt about your relationship with a soon-to-be married man. Because I must admit, I didn't think you had it in you.'

Her cheeks burned with shame at being likened to some harlot but what could she say that wouldn't break a confidence. 'His fiancée's a bitch.'

He leaned back and laced fingers behind his head. 'Of course she is. They always are.'

His expression was inscrutable. Was he laughing at her? Because her comment was trite. How many others also tried to explain away their actions with the same feeble excuse. But this was different, Sasha was a total cow.

'He's not happy and I'm offering him an outlet for his misery.' Rodriguez raised his eyebrow but remained silent. She was aware of digging an enormous hole for herself but didn't know what else to say. 'It's only until the end of the cruise and then we go our separate ways. There's not much more to say.'

He shuffled forwards and gently took her hands in his. 'Do you know what you're doing?'

'Yeeeeessss.'

'That doesn't sound very confident.'

She straightened up. 'Yes, I know what I'm doing. I care for him but we both know the relationship comes to an end in a few days' time.'

'I'm glad to hear it. All I'm saying, he paid a hell of a lot of money for your fairytale night in the penthouse.'

Her mouth dropped open. 'H-how d-did you know about that?'

'Not much gets past me, sweetie.'

He was watching her intently, but she wouldn't look at him. He was wrong. She did know what she was doing. She was in control. Tony knew the score. Everything was fine.

'Okay, I've told you mine.' She gave him a hard stare in case he tried to back out. 'You need to tell me yours.'

He nodded and went over to the bar, but this time brought back a photo album. 'Bunch up, skinny bum.' She scooted across the sofa to allow a sizeable gap for Rodriguez to lower himself next to her. 'Now I'm only divulging this to you in the strictest confidence because Louis likes you. And because you can carry off a pair of penguin slippers almost as well as me.'

She nodded solemnly, not believing it for a moment. It was an obvious excuse. Deal or no deal, he clearly wanted to tell the story and she eagerly flicked through the pages, laughing at much younger and thinner images of him. There were a multitude of group shots with colleagues on various cruise ships. Everyone was smiling and appeared to be having a great time. Sebastian had barely changed, always the dapper chap in metal-framed spectacles.

'Seb and I have worked together on the same cruise ships for over twenty-five years. Back in the day, I was the understudy and Seb always won the FFFC trophy. But he did it with integrity. It was a bit of fun and nobody got hurt.' Rodriguez took the album and flicked to the last page. In the photo, there were three figures – Rodriguez, Sebastian and another young man. Smooth faced and gorgeous.

'Who's that?'

'That's Matthias.' Rodriguez stared at the photo intently. 'Do you know what I excel at?'

'Making people laugh,' Agnes answered immediately, and he nodded.

'Do you know what I'm terrible at?'

'Losing.' Again, the answer was immediate, and he chuckled.

'Yes, that's true. But it's relationships. I'm too selfish. I'm too vain. I have unbelievably high expectations and want everything done my way.' He looked across at her. 'Feel free to jump in any time and disagree with me.' She smiled and shook her head, so he carried on. 'Oh yes, I can make people laugh and that's incredibly attractive and a highly effective seduction tool. Who doesn't love to be entertained? But it's always the same story. After a few weeks, or if I'm lucky I might make it to three months, the novelty wears off and all my relationships go into terminal decline.'

Agnes nibbled her pizza and listened as Rodriguez described how he became obsessed with winning the FFFC but also grew increasingly jealous of anyone who could sustain a relationship. On the last cruise of one particular season, Matthias boarded. He was on holiday with his family and Sebastian selected him. It was obvious to everyone that Sebastian was in love with Matthias and the attraction was mutual. From day one they were together as much as possible and as Sebastian was a waiter, Matthias hung around the restaurants. Agnes could sense a looming 'but' approaching. The story was not going to end well, but she kept quiet as Rodriguez explained that he realised there was only one sure way to win.

He told Matthias about the FFFC and made out that Sebastian was using him. The man was heartbroken and angry. A combination Rodriguez used to his full advantage. He repeatedly bedded Matthias and lifted the trophy. Sebastian in turn hated Rodriguez for what he'd done.

'Sebastian wasn't scoring points from Matthias, was he?' Agnes asked and scrutinised the photo more closely. It was a natural shot; the three men had been caught off guard. Rodriguez was mid-flow, presumably telling a joke, and the other two were laughing. It was a lovely photo of what appeared to be great mates.

Rodriguez shook his head. 'No, he had taken the same stance as you. Matthias was more important than a stupid game. But back then I was consumed with envy at their relationship, at any relationship, so I deliberately broke Seb's heart. All I wanted to do was win and destroy others' happiness.'

'And now?'

The entertainer's mask slipped to reveal a harrowed expression, no longer the bringer of jollity but a man in pain. A lonely man. 'I wish with all my heart I could go back and change what I did. Seb's a great guy and deserves somebody special. He deserves to be happy, so rightfully takes potshots at me because I took it away from him. And because I'm a bitch I respond. I don't deserve to be happy, and my penance is to bring joy by making others laugh.'

A fresh set of tears rolled down Agnes's face. 'That's such a sad thing to say. I'm sure you'll find happiness.'

He cast his arms wide. 'This is my little cocoon of happiness, darling. Here and during those brief hours I'm entertaining others.'

Her metal spoon scraped the last dregs of an I've-died-and-gone-to-heaven tiramisu, and it enabled her to reach a decision. 'Can you withdraw me from the FFFC, please?'

'Are you sure about this? You'll be giving up first place.' He picked up his mobile and composed a message. 'Once I send this there's no going back.'

She carefully placed her plate down on the glass table. 'Yes, it's the right thing to do.'

'Okay, the message has been sent. You're no longer in the FFFC and neither am I.'

Her spoon clattered onto the empty plate and bounced onto the cream carpet. Luckily it was licked clean. 'B-but isn't it what you thrive at? Isn't it what you live for?'

'And that's exactly why I should no longer be in it,' Rodriguez replied and then winked. 'Besides, keeping scores is truly horrific. Let some other sap take on the challenge. I'm far too old for all that bullshit.'

Chapter Twenty-Three

Freshly brewed coffee and warm bread. An intoxicating aroma that transported her back home. She half expected to open her eyes and find her father and stepmother chatting and giggling in the kitchen as her three half-brothers tore around the house pretending to be pirates. But sadly, those days were long gone. Her neck and shoulders ached from a night on the sofa. They'd talked into the early hours and, tucked under a snugly warm blanket, Rodriguez had revealed a softer side that Agnes believed few people were permitted to see. The last thing she remembered was closing her eyes while listening to the *Little House on the Prairie* signature tune.

She peeled open gritty eyes to find Rodriguez sitting opposite in white jeans and a billowing harlequin smock top. 'Wakey-wakey, sleepy head.'

'Shit, what's the time?' She sat bolt upright, still wearing a pink dressing gown. The penguin slippers were nowhere to be seen.

'Never fear, you've got twenty minutes till you're needed in the galley. Plenty of time to enjoy your breakfast.' She scrambled to her feet, but he motioned for her to sit down. 'There's a clean uniform hanging up for you in the bathroom, and I took an early stroll along the top deck this morning to have a chat with a very pleasant young man.'

'You went and met Tony?' Her brain was a foggy haze, desperately craving more sleep. 'Why didn't you wake me up?'

'Because you were wrecked, my dear.' He moved the candles on the glass table till they were perfectly aligned. 'I must admit he wasn't what I expected.'

Agnes spread a thick layer of apricot jam on her still warm bread. 'What do you mean?'

'Well, I know he's engaged, and I know he slapped Maria's backside for a bet, and I know he toddles around with the rest of his mates in awe of the alpha-male, who up until recently was earning Bettina plenty of points. So I had him pegged as a mindless sheep or a dutiful chick following its leader's ever beck and call. I reckoned he mustn't have much get up and go about him and couldn't have many morals if he's shagging someone behind the love of his life's back.'

'And now?' She was keen to hear what could possibly follow that succinct character assassination.

'He improves on closer inspection.'

Agnes brightened. 'Yes, he does, doesn't he.'

'Some people appear assholes at first, but you realise they aren't. Whereas in my case, the more you get to know me, the more you discover I am one.'

Agnes waited for the punchline but realised he was being deadly serious. She brushed her fingers free of breadcrumbs and scowled. 'But that's not true. I don't mind admitting that I've skirted around you for the last few years. You've got a razor-sharp wit that cuts people to ribbons. And if people don't hit your unbelievably high expectations, your legendary temper is unleashed. You're funny and incredibly intimidating at the same time. But last night you let me in, and it was lovely.' She twisted her fingers together. 'I now consider you a friend and I hope you see me as one too.'

He sat quietly as an art-deco wall clock ticked, but a smile twitched at his lips. 'I like you, Agnes. And I don't say that about many people. You're welcome to wear my penguin slippers anytime.' She smiled but it faltered as he cleared his throat in a rather serious manner. 'I only chatted to Tony briefly but it's obvious that he's smitten on you. Be careful there. You might think you're in control, but that rarely happens when emotions get in the way. People don't cope very well with having their hearts broken. Are you strong enough to cope with the possible fallout?' But then he dismissively waved his hand in the air and there was a twinkle in his eye. 'But what would I know about any of that. My track record is abysmal. Now get to work or Louis will kill me. And besides, I need to catch up on my beauty sleep. I'm giving myself the morning off. Nobody will say anything, they wouldn't dare. After all, I'm the great and temperamental Rodriguez.'

***

It was eleven o'clock in the morning and Agnes had already consumed three nuclear-grade expressos to wake up. With so much caffeine pumping around her body, she was jittery and couldn't stop talking. Usually, she said very little, except 'yes, chef' and 'no, chef' but today she kept rambling on and on. After a couple of hours, she was pulled to one side and half expected to be ordered to shut up or interrogated for drug use. But it was neither. Somebody wished to talk to her.

She stepped into the service corridor and came face to face with a sheepish Maria.

'I'm at work, what do you want?' Agnes was in no mood for niceties.

'I saw you'd withdrawn from the FFFC, and I've spoken to Rodriguez.'

'And?' She wasn't going to make it easy for her friend.

'I'm so sorry, I-I thought you wanted to win as much as me. And I stupidly thought that you'd been too busy to input your scores but … but you wouldn't have forgotten if you truly wanted to win.'

Agnes crossed her arms tightly. 'No, I wouldn't have. I can't believe you input scores on my behalf. Why did you go behind my back? Friends don't do that. I'm still livid with you.'

'Please forgive me,' Maria begged and tugged at Agnes's sleeve. 'If you want the truth, I wasn't thinking about you, I was thinking that I'd want to win if it was me. But you've got integrity, whereas I don't.'

Rodriguez's voice floated into her wired brain. Agnes had already worked out if Rodriguez wasn't to blame it had to be Maria who'd forwarded the points because nobody else knew about her and Tony. But he'd counselled her to go easy on the talented photographer because, after all, she'd organised Agnes and Tony's secret penthouse liaison and that had to be worth something.

'You look like shit,' Agnes muttered.

'As soon as I saw Rodriguez's message yesterday evening, I went to our cabin and stayed awake all night, waiting for you to come back.'

Agnes leaned against the wall and closed her eyes. 'I was beyond furious with you and knew it was better to stay away.' She felt Maria beside her and slowly opened her eyes. 'Thank you for organising the other night.'

Maria perked up. 'I thought it'd be nice for the two of you to have a touch of luxury. Our cabin is hardly romantic, and you can't risk using his. I'd been commissioned to take a series of photos of the couple staying in the penthouse suite. They wanted to document their golden wedding anniversary cruise but unfortunately a family crisis meant they had to fly home early from Split. As it was empty, I figured why not make use of it? It only took a little bit of coaxing to get it organised.'

'By that, you mean bribing people?'

Maria shrugged. 'Nobody does anything for free. I negotiated a price and Tony paid it.'

Agnes chewed her lower lip. 'Was it very expensive?'

'All I'll say is Tony is either loaded or he likes you a lot. Nobody has ever spent that much money on me for one night. I hope it was worth it?'

Rodriguez's and Maria's combined comments unsettled her stomach, but she dismissed them. No, her churning insides were caused by copious amounts of caffeine and nothing to do with Tony's strengthening affections. 'It was amazing. I think that'll be the closest I ever come to luxury living.' Agnes sighed. 'Anyway, why are you so wet?'

Maria patted her short sodden hair, and a puddle was forming around her soggy trainers. 'Oh yes, you wouldn't know, being stuck inside. We've had the mother of all storms.'

She pulled out her camera and played video footage taken from the top deck. The Italian port of Taranto was barely visible through a wall of water and the sound of rain thundering on metal was incredible. In fact, it wasn't rain at all but hailstones and made the deck look like it had a bad case of dandruff. In the background was the muffled chatter of passengers and then a rumble of thunder that slowly built to a crescendo. Maria cycled through stunning images of lightning strikes over the imposing Castello Aragonese fortress.

'I think you're going to be just fine being a travel photographer,' Agnes declared. 'You could easily sell those.'

Maria smiled. 'Are we okay then? Have you forgiven me?'

'Yes, we're fine and yes, you're forgiven. I'm not in the FFFC anymore so my conscience is clear. We dock in Valletta the day after tomorrow and I intend to make the most of Tony till then. But I had better get back to work or I won't be going anywhere.'

Chapter Twenty-Four

The pamphlet that had been thrust into his hand by an enthusiastic shop owner declared Alberobello to be one of Italy's most romantic destinations. And, standing on one of its narrow streets, surrounded by iconic trulli, who could argue? The UNESCO World Heritage site was packed with these beautiful white houses topped with unique conical stone roofs. Tony could hear the knowledgeable guide inform their group that the unusual design had been born out of a historic way to evade taxes. That'd be right. Back in the day, hadn't people in the UK blocked up windows to avoid paying window tax? And if there'd been an Italian tax on rooftops, why wouldn't enterprising folk construct a roof that could be taken down before the tax inspector called?

Jahmar had come up trumps again with his Valle d'Itria tour. They'd already enjoyed the pretty hilltop town of Locorotondo, and the final stop would be the cute village of Martina Franca. Coming inland had been a good move. The skies towards Taranto were ominous and Tony hoped the weather would clear before their city tour later that day.

Patrick sidled up to him. 'I reckon Sebastian would love it here, don't you?'

Tony smiled. 'I reckon Agnes would as well.' There'd been a no-holds-barred confessional by both men after their unexpected meeting in the corridor. Patrick knew about Agnes and Tony knew about Sebastian. 'Maybe we can all come back here one day?'

'That would be nice.' Patrick double-checked none of their group was within earshot. 'Have you spoken to her yet about the future? You're running out of time, son.'

'Part of me wants to and the other part doesn't.' They were walking uphill between two rows of trulli. Lights were suspended overhead with straw hats and baskets dangling down. Tony wasn't quite sure what that was all about, and their guide was too far away to ask. Tourists sauntered past, window shopping or sitting outside to enjoy Puglia's mouth watering produce. 'Our time together is so precious that I don't want to spoil it. Agnes was very insistent on the short-term nature of our relationship, and I don't think she's a woman who changes her mind easily.'

'But you won't know, unless you ask.' Patrick stressed the ludicrously obvious truth. 'You held back all those years with Sasha and look where that got you.'

'I know you're right—'

'Hey, you two, get a move on,' Jahmar called from the church steps of St. Antonio. 'We've got plenty more to see.'

Tony acknowledged him with a wave. 'I'll tell her tonight. Like you said, I'm running out of time, and I've already wasted so much of it with Sasha.'

Patrick's face crinkled into an enormous grin. 'Go for it, son. What have you got to lose?'

Chapter Twenty-Five

It was the penultimate evening and the galley crew had outdone themselves. The first two courses were exceptional and then the lights dimmed and out came all the waiting staff carrying aloft a procession of flaming baked Alaska. The dining room was lit up by flickering flames and hundreds of illuminated mobile screens. At the very front was Sebastian, and Patrick tracked his every move, hardly daring to breathe. The maître d' came to their table and ceremoniously placed the dessert in the middle. He handed a knife to Tony and winked. 'Would sir care to do the honours?'

***

If he'd been at home, Tony would have unbuttoned his trousers. He was absolutely stuffed and shook his head at the offer of tea or coffee. Perhaps Agnes could massage his stomach later. He casually checked his watch. It was time to make a move.

'If nobody minds, I think I'll take a stroll around the deck to wear off this delicious meal.'

'You get yourself away, lad.' Patrick spoke for them all.

'Actually, can I have a word?' Tony's heart dropped at Jahmar's request, but what could he do except nod? They walked a few paces away. 'There's someone I'd like you to meet, do you mind?'

'No not at all.' Tony flicked his eyes towards Patrick, who was closely watching them. 'Give me one second.' He walked back to the table.

'What do you want me to tell her?' Patrick whispered.

'I've got caught up with Jahmar. I don't know how long I'm going to be because he wants me to meet his new girlfriend.' His mind was racing. What should he do for the best? 'I'll meet her in the usual place in an hour but if I'm not there tell her to leave and I'll go to her cabin later.'

He rejoined Jahmar. 'Come on then, lover boy, let's go meet the woman who's finally captured your heart.'

'Will you please be nice to her?' Jahmar muttered nervously. 'Don't make me out to be a total dickhead and don't tell too many embarrassing stories. And don't mention how I've never been in love. And don't—'

They were in the atrium, beneath the grand staircase and surrounded by high-end boutiques. Tony bustled Jahmar past the store he'd hired his tuxedo from and into the art gallery.

'Get a grip, will you,' Tony instructed and appraised his friend. He brushed down the Saville Row jacket and straightened the silk tie. 'Show me your teeth and tilt your head back. Excellent, you've got no food trapped or bogies on display. We're good to go.' He nodded to a bemused Vlad and marched Jahmar back outside.

'Thanks for that.' Jahmar began to take deep breaths. 'I don't want to mess this up. You're the first one of us she's met.'

'I'm honoured. Do I get to know anything about her first? Like maybe a name?'

'Oh yes. Her name is Celeste. She's French, twenty-four and is one of the beauticians aboard.'

'And how did you meet?' Tony smirked. 'Did she wax your unbelievably hairy shoulders? Because that'd put the fear of God into any woman.'

'Ha, ha, very funny. If you must know we met when she gave me a facial with beard and eyebrow trim.'

'Heaven forbid you miss your monthly spa treatment, and how very handy for you to be dating a beautician.'

They were heading along the corridor by the dance studio. 'And what's that supposed to mean?'

'Your annual grooming outgoings are probably larger than some small countries' GDP. You'll save an absolute fortune if this holiday shag develops into something more.'

'That's exactly the 1950s male chauvinistic crap you are forbidden from uttering,' Jahmar snapped.

'Good grief, you have got it bad.' What a turn up for the books. Here he was trying to instil confidence in Jahmar, while naturally winding him up at the same time. For as long as he could remember, it'd always been the other way around. Nevertheless, he held up his hands and grinned. 'I'm joking. Honestly, give me some credit. As I recall, you're usually the one to spout sexist nonsense, not me.'

They were at the glass doors to the spa and Jahmar took a deep breath as he pushed them open.

'Hey, gorgeous,' he purred, and a slender blonde woman sprung off her chair, squealed with delight and flew into Jahmar's outstretched arms.

Tony looked away as the pair reacquainted themselves with each other's tonsils. 'I can always leave if you'd like.'

'But no, don't be so silly,' Celeste replied and planted a kiss on both of his cheeks. 'I'm honoured that my gorgeous Jahmar has finally introduced me to his bestest friend and soon-to-be brother-in-law. I feel like I know you already.' She dropped her voice, and it tickled in Tony's ear. 'You must promise to tell me lots of embarrassing stories about him.'

Jahmar swept her up and spun her around. 'He's already been warned, so you're out of luck.'

She put on a mock sad face and then laughed. It was light-hearted and happy. 'But I want to hear all about how you grew up together and were young bucks roaming around London. That is surely not off limits?'

'Oh, I think that can be arranged,' Tony replied. He instantly liked her. She was a breath of fresh air, bursting with joy. He watched as Jahmar kissed her nose and she grabbed his face and gave him a full-on smacker. An unembarrassed you're-my-man-and-I-don't-care-who-knows-it kiss. His eyes shone when she looked at him. Maybe there was more to this one than all the others. 'Celeste, you might just have what it takes to keep this hairy-shouldered bloke in line.'

Jahmar looked utterly appalled, but she roared with laughter. 'I never thought a man could have so much hair on any part of his body other than his head. But it's true. He's my gorgeous, loveable hairy creature, and I don't want any other.' She linked arms with them. 'Come, my English men, the night is young and so are we. Let us enjoy every minute of the time we're given.'

Chapter Twenty-Six

It was after midnight and Agnes was fuming. Where the hell was he? She paced back and forth in the cramped confines of her cabin. She'd waited on deck at the appointed time. He hadn't shown and then the heavens had opened, driving everyone indoors. She had nowhere else to go. She'd been half tempted to knock on Rodriguez's cabin door, but felt embarrassed to do so. The penultimate night of any cruise was always the busiest. He would be the centre of attention. Guests always wanted photographs with him and would exchange email addresses with promises to return the next year. And amazingly many did. No wonder management loved the flamboyant Canadian. He was a star. An outrageously funny, say it how it is, hold your sides with laughter kind of guy. No wonder he lived to be on stage. He'd told her that many passengers skipped the last night show. It was as if they knew things were coming to an end and wanted to retire to their cabins and pack their suitcases, ready to depart bright and early the next day. Was it because the last full day of the cruise was at sea? Agnes would have thought that was even more reason to go out with a bang.

They'd pulled anchor from Taranto earlier in the evening and wouldn't strike land again until the day after tomorrow. Maria always grumbled. The last full day at sea was a pain in the butt. It was by far and away the busiest day for the ship's photographers, as passengers wanted mementos, snapshots with their new friends. The kitchens were flat out as guests ate their fill, declaring the diet would start once they got home, before stuffing one last chocolate éclair down their gullets. The spa was always fully booked, and the exorbitantly priced shops did a roaring trade as passengers suddenly realised they needed to buy that gift for work, girlfriend, boyfriend or spouse. For all everyone thought they were different, humans were very predictable, and each cruise followed a similar pattern.

At 00:34 there was a loud rapping on the cabin door. She flung the door open, and an inebriated Tony tumbled onto the floor. She watched with increasing irritability as he crawled and giggled his way over to the table and chairs and heaved himself upwards.

'Hey, baby,' he slurred. 'Fancy a quickie?'

Agnes was supremely unimpressed. 'I don't think you could get it up if you tried.'

He was unbelievably affronted and staggered to his feet, fumbling with his flies before giving up. He then began a slurred retelling of the night's adventures. And the more he talked and staggered around the cabin the more incensed she became. Eventually, just as she was going to blow her top and kick him out, he collapsed onto the bottom bunk. Fifteen seconds later the sound of snoring filled the air and continued long after she'd finished slamming cupboard doors.

Chapter Twenty-Seven

A dull thud from the corridor woke him, swiftly followed by a sharp searing pain. He touched his head to make sure some sadist wasn't attacking it with a chainsaw. He cracked open his eyes but there was no difference. Eyes closed, eyes open and still pitch black. Where the hell was the porthole and a lovely view of the ever-stretching Med? And then, bit by bit the previous night trickled into his consciousness. Fleeting visions of laughing and chatting with Jahmar and Celeste, knocking back beer, cocktails and then downing lines of shots at various bars. More visions slunk into his fragile mind and this time on a dancefloor. The three of them creating an ever-widening space as fellow dancers cleared the vicinity to avoid a whirling, spinning mass of arms and legs. And the scene changed again, and this time he was staggering about Agnes's cabin drunk, regaling her with how much Jahmar and Celeste adored one another. He recalled being met with a face that could curdle milk.

He groaned and dropped his head back on the pillow as he remembered his pièce de resistance: standing in the middle of the floor, swaying dangerously with arms outstretched and telling her that all night he'd answered Celeste's questions about Sasha. And when he'd replied about how wonderful it was to be in love, how fantastic it was to be with the woman of his dreams, to have a true connection and know you'd grow old together, he hadn't been talking about Jahmar's sister. He'd been talking about Agnes. And then he'd face-planted the bottom bunk.

He lay there in the darkness, recalling Patrick's voice.

'You're running out of time, son. You won't know unless you tell her.'

Well, he'd told her now. Fumbling about in the darkness, he located his mobile and with the faint beam managed to clamber out of the bunk and gingerly stood upright. The reverberations from the engine rattled his brain further. They were much louder, down in the bowels of the ship, than in his cabin. He just managed to make it to the toilet before throwing up. Wiping his mouth, he flicked the light on and winced at the brightness but almost sobbed with gratitude. There on the table was a bottle of water and a box of painkillers. He swallowed two tablets and downed half the water while reading her note.

I figured you might need these. See you later. Agnes x

He took it as a good sign. She clearly didn't hate his guts. Or at least felt sorry enough to come to his aid. It was still too early to go back to his cabin. He didn't fancy walking in on the lovebirds and instead stepped onto the bottom bunk and peered at an insight into Agnes's life. They'd talked at length about losing their fathers and how it had changed them both. Him forced to turn his back on art and enter an interminably dull existence as an IT specialist and Agnes still angry at her father's drunken actions that had cut short his life. It had further stoked the burning desire to leave her hometown and make it as a Head Chef.

The walls and ceiling were covered in photos, doodles, postcards, paintings and drawings. He caught sight of her as a child sitting proud on a pony. A man smiled at the camera. They both had the same curved nose and grey-green eyes. It had to be her father. And the same man laughed with a woman at a kitchen table with three young boys parading around with a Jolly Roger flag, toy scabbards and eye patches. There were plenty of photos of Agnes cooking and baking with the same woman. That must be her stepmother. But the greatest number were during her time on board. There were snapshots with Maria in various locations, in the kitchen, and lots with a group of six others. He recognised Sebastian, Vlad, Bettina, Maria, and the hilarious large guy in stiletto boots and a catsuit was the ship's comedian extraordinaire. He'd had a nice chat with Rodriguez on the top deck yesterday morning. It sounded like Agnes and him had enjoyed quite a night. He'd have to ask her about it later. Taking another sip of blessed water, he glanced at the photos and hoped that soon there'd be ones of him and Agnes together.

Had he blown it last night? The note suggested not but he'd pretty much declared his undying love for her. But he could pass it off as being drunk. He staggered over to the mirror and appraised himself. What did Agnes see when she looked at him? He patted his crumpled shirt. Almost two weeks of fine dining was starting to show, and he sucked his tummy in. Just as well he wasn't going to have to worry about getting into a wedding suit. He was average height, average build, average looking. A face made slightly more interesting by stubble which hid his acne scars. He wasn't anything to write home about but then looks weren't everything.

He slumped down on the chair. What was he doing? What was he thinking? Was Agnes right? Was he really searching for the happy-ever-after with her because he couldn't have it with Sasha? No. He stood up abruptly. That was defeatism. Him and Agnes had a connection. Things were going to work out.

Chapter Twenty-Eight

Agnes aggressively chopped vegetables and dumped them in a colander while colleagues warily glanced her way. She'd made no eye contact with anyone so far this morning and was too consumed with anger to speak. She'd graciously left Tony the water, painkillers and even a note with a kiss. But she wanted to scream at him. Their penultimate night and he'd ruined it by getting so drunk he could barely stand … and in the company of Celeste! The woman was a blabbermouth of the highest order. At least he'd kept his trap shut about their dalliance. She grabbed an onion, and the sharp blade diced it easily, and then another and another. The fluid motion usually calmed her but not today.

She'd warned him they were nothing more than a bit of fun. An exciting holiday romance till the end of the cruise. He'd agreed to that but then he'd gone and broken the rules by slurring his undying love for her. The knife slipped and she cursed at almost nicking her finger. She should have known better than to get involved. She'd sensed he liked her, that he was too attached. But she'd let lust get in the way of reason. She grabbed a handful of carrots and the gleaming knife made short work of them. But there was more to it than that. Tony Acebi was under her skin. She'd confided in him about her father and her family. Something she hadn't done with anyone else. And she wanted him to do well. To ditch the bitch of a fiancée and follow his dreams. She paused midway through dissecting a cabbage and stared at the kitchen wall. Yes, she wanted him to be happy, but it couldn't be with her. There was no room in her life for any distractions. She was going to be a Head Chef on a cruise ship within three years, come what may.

***

The final full day of the cruise and nobody seemed to be that eager to get up early. Tony skulked around what seemed an unusually quiet ship, window shopped, grabbed a coffee and stared at the horizon from the Mariners cocktail lounge until he deemed it safe to go back to his cabin. There was no sign of Jahmar or Celeste so after a quick shower and in fresh clothes he set off to find everyone else. His mates were at breakfast (except Patrick) and Jahmar was, as usual, holding court.

'And he finally decides to show up,' Jahmar called across the dining room. 'I've just been telling the lads about last night. My God, you look like hell.'

Tony sat down carefully. 'It's far worse inside my head and I've already taken two lots of painkillers this morning.'

The rest of the breakfast passed off without incident and while everyone discussed what to do that day, Tony made his excuses with the mother of all hangovers. Everyone nodded, they'd all been there. But that wasn't the real reason. The huge ship was suddenly too small. Too confining. He paced the deck countless times, traipsed around the shops, took in a movie but it was the confines of his head he couldn't escape from, and the final scene with Agnes replayed itself.

Two women.

One he didn't want and the other he ached for with every fibre in his body. Sasha still hadn't rung. Oh yes, she'd apologised to her brother after he kicked off at her for leaving the cats. But she hadn't contacted who she believed was still her fiancée, which spoke volumes about their fractured relationship. How hadn't he noticed her gross lack of affection before? How had he got to the point of almost tying himself to her before realising it would be a terrible mistake? Even with all the hints dropped by his mum and sisters.

And then there was Agnes.

He'd done what Patrick had suggested and laid his cards on the table. Okay, being totally pissed at the time had been stupid and it hadn't been the way he'd wanted to do it. But surely, she felt the same way? How could she want to walk away tomorrow? Call a halt to what they had and could have? Everywhere he turned, couples were in love. And it made him more determined to make things right tonight. He'd explain himself properly.

Everything was going to be fine.

The fresh air was marginally helping his throbbing head and he peered through the Mariners cocktail lounge window to see all his mates drinking. He couldn't face the smell of alcohol right now so decided to retire to the stern with his sketch pad. The weather was cooler now. Billowing clouds raced across the sky and most of the passengers preferred the warmth of indoors. He pulled up a chair and set to work. A few hours later, he was fairly happy with the results. A movement caught his eye and he quickly flipped over the paper and put the finishing touches to a seascape.

'Not bad.' Jahmar peered at the sketchpad. He was wrapped up in a fleece and wearing an enormous grin. He passed across a steaming hot cup of tea and settled down next to him. 'Something to warm your cockles.'

'Hello, you two.' It was Celeste, bundled up in one of Jahmar's designer hoodies. 'I'm on a short break and thought I'd come to find you both.' She straddled her boyfriend and chuckled as he whispered sweet nothings in her ear.

'Will you two get a room,' Tony grumbled.

'Your friend is missing his fiancée, I think?' Celeste joked but froze as Bettina strolled past. 'Whore.'

Tony frowned, convinced he'd misheard. 'What did you say, Celeste?'

'That woman is a whore. She used my baby.' Celeste tickled Jahmar's beard. 'But her loss is my gain.'

Jahmar shifted uneasily. 'What do you mean "used"? I only had a few dates with her. She was a bit boring actually. But you know all this. Remember what we said – no secrets.'

Celeste tilted her head. 'The woman is cruel. You're better off without her.' There was a harshness in her voice that Tony had never heard before. It spoke of an untold history between the pair. He wondered what had gone on.

She slid off Jahmar, but he pulled her back. 'What aren't you telling me?'

Celeste slowly sat down and dropped her voice, forcing both men to lean forward. 'There's a league. It's called the FFFC. Members score points by bedding passengers. Bettina picked you, baby. I heard her say you weren't worth the points. I'm sorry. And I-I think that maybe …' Celeste's voice was barely a whisper as her eyes glistened with tears. 'I think they gain points from sleeping with colleagues as well.'

'Is your ex-boyfriend, Vlad, in this league by any chance?' Jahmar growled and Celeste slowly nodded as her lip trembled. He stood up, the pulse in his neck throbbing. 'I won't be long.'

'What do you know about this FFFC?' Tony asked, as uneasiness settled in his stomach. Jahmar was undoubtedly off to confront Vlad, to defend his girlfriend's honour. He should probably go after him. There was also a strong probability Jahmar would confront Bettina next, to find out if he'd been part of a sordid game. The bloke had been smitten with the woman regardless of his protestations. There was no denying Bettina and Celeste looked remarkably alike. Maybe that was at the root of Celeste's dislike. Nobody wanted to be second choice.

Celeste was staring at the door Jahmar had disappeared through, as if deciding whether to follow, but turned and shrugged. 'Not much, I only got a glance at Vlad's phone a few times.' Her eyes furtively shifted across the deck, and he understood she'd been snooping. 'I saw a league table and a thread of congratulatory messages with tips and tricks on how to get the best out of players like finding common hobbies. I can't remember all the names but there was definitely Vlad, Bettina, my friend Maria and her room-mate Agnes. And then I overheard Bettina and put two and two together. My baby never stood a chance.'

Tony shot upright so fast that Celeste jumped in her seat. 'I'd better go and make sure Jahmar doesn't do anything stupid.'

He was barely aware of Celeste mumbling her thanks as he raced along the deck. But he wasn't going after his mate. He was after Agnes.

Chapter Twenty-Nine

The clock finally ticked around to finishing time. Agnes waved a cheery goodbye and headed for the door. As the day progressed, her anger had evaporated until she finally saw the funny side of last night's debacle (much to her colleagues' relief). Tony had drunk one too many and had probably spent most of the day suffering from a horrific hangover and acute embarrassment. The bloke was on holiday after all, privately dealing with his long-term relationship falling apart and on top of that had to endure an evening with his ex-fiancée's brother who was loved-up with one of the most annoyingly upbeat members of the crew. No wonder he'd knocked them back and probably couldn't even remember his protestations of love.

She grinned and opened the door. It was their last night together and it was going to go out with a bang and not a whimper. This would be a holiday he'd never forget.

***

He registered her smiling face a fraction before she spotted him and then her grin faltered and vanished.

'W-what's wrong?'

Her voice was full of concern, but he knew her for what she was and what she was capable of. Pure hatred radiated off his body. He could barely hold it together enough to form a sentence. But he wanted her to know.

'It was all an act, wasn't it?' He was right up in her face, and he saw confusion reflected in her eyes, but it was a ploy. 'I know about the FFFC.'

There was a sharp intake of breath, and she stepped back, but he grabbed her wrist and dragged her through a door emblazoned 'No Entry'. It was a service corridor and the harsh lighting projected dark shadows across her shocked face.

'H-how did … how did you …' She stopped and tried to compose herself. He hated her even more for that. For stalling, buying time to come up with more lies. 'Who told you about the FFFC? What do you know?'

'It was Celeste.' He saw a flicker of recognition in her eyes and the rage ramped up further. There was no way she could deny it. 'She saw the members' names with messages on Vlad's phone and then overheard Bettina talking to herself, saying Jahmar wasn't worth the points.' And again, those grey-green eyes betrayed her. They widened ever so slightly before she slumped against the wall. 'Your name was on the list, Agnes. A member of a sordid little club that beds passengers. That strings them along, plays with their emotions and doesn't give a toss about what it does to them.'

'It's not what you think.' Her voice implored him to understand.

And he got it loud and clear. He was attracted to women who couldn't give a shit. Women who used and abused others. They manipulated him, lied and cheated, killed his dreams, kept him in a cage. They laughed and sniggered about him behind his back. At the spineless, downtrodden Tony who never stood up for himself, who took all the crap they dished out and kept coming back for more. Who was pathetically grateful for their attention. His body shook. His head pounded with fury. Somebody needed to pay for what they'd done to him, otherwise he'd explode.

'Was it worth it?' he hissed, like steam released under great pressure. It did nothing to diminish the white-hot rage. He could barely see straight. Their bodies were pressed up against one another, as he used his weight to pin her against the wall. But the attraction was gone. There was nothing but repulsion. 'Come on, Agnes. How about it?' He fumbled to undo his flies and pressed her hand against his crotch. She tried to pull it away, but he kept it firmly in place. 'Oh yes, baby that feels good.' He forced her hand to massage him. 'How many points is this worth? Or I've got an even better idea. What about a blowjob?'

He grabbed her shoulders, pressing downwards with all his might until the pressure buckled her knees. He grabbed her head with both hands and pressed it into his crotch. She desperately kept twisting her head away, pushing her hands against his legs, begging him to stop. But he couldn't. He shut out the protests and forced her head forwards and still she fought him.

'What's this, you don't fancy it?' He sneered, glowering at the cowering figure beneath him. 'Not in the mood? Or is it not as much fun WHEN THE VICTIM KNOWS WHAT YOU'RE UP TO?'

He screamed out the last few words and they echoed along the corridor as he cast her aside and she slumped to the floor. She was nothing but filthy rubbish, the sort that collected on the water in the forgotten corners of each port they'd docked at. It was left there to slowly break down and decay, useless and worthless to everyone.

He stepped back and zipped up his flies as she knelt crying on the hard metal floor. He was repulsed by the very sight of her with tears and snot running down her face.

'It wasn't like that, Tony.'

'I don't want to hear your pathetic excuses.' He spat out the words. 'Was it because I'm not much of a looker, a bit of a pushover? Is that why you picked me from the countless others? Did you think I'd be flattered by the attention? You must have thought you'd won the lottery when I was terrified on that horse, when you found out my father had died and when I confessed to giving up my dreams of being an artist. I was a sitting duck, wasn't I?'

She clambered to her feet, and he was vaguely amused to see anger in her face.

'I picked you because you were a sexist male chauvinist pig who thought they had the right to slap a woman's arse,' she screamed back at him. 'You saw Maria as nothing more than property you owned and were entitled to do with her as you wished. That's why I chose you. Look at your own behaviour before you judge others.'

'I'm so glad you have such high standards,' he jeered. 'But I am judging you, Agnes. You continued to play the game long after you knew what I was really like. Long after I apologised. Long after you knew … that I'd fallen in love with you.' He hadn't meant for it to come out like that, just like he hadn't meant for the tears of hurt and shame to stream down his face. 'You made me believe in myself again. You made me see myself for what I'd become and what my life was going to be if I didn't make a change. You made me realise I didn't want to marry Sasha and wanted to be an artist. You've reignited my passion for art which I thought had been totally obliterated. And now I can't switch it off. And I hate you for that, Agnes Karapetsa. I really hate you.' He slid down the wall and curled up into a ball. She might have said *sorry* before leaving or it could easily have been *I hate you too.* He wasn't sure, because everything was drowned out by his own sobbing at what could never be. And to discover it hadn't been real. It had been a game to her and nothing more.

Chapter Thirty

Strong legs carried her swiftly to safety – along the service corridor, out into the public areas, through the staff-only quarters and into her cell. Maybe monks and nuns had the right idea: pare back all your belongings, relinquish physical wants and lead a simple life. She got changed and climbed into bed, clutching her teddy, and turned off the light. But the utter blackness couldn't shut out the horrific encounter with Tony that replayed itself. She curled up even tighter, wanting to blot it all out. But of course, she couldn't.

The light flicked on, but she lay motionless. Maybe if she kept quiet …

'I know you're there,' Maria called out. 'I've had messages from Vlad and Bettina. I know about Jahmar and Tony and the FFFC.'

Red-eyed Agnes peeked over the bunk. 'What happened?'

Maria pulled down the chair and flopped into it. 'Jahmar had a go at Vlad for sleeping with Celeste for a bet. He promptly laughed in his face and said Celeste was only bitter after being dumped because she'd been caught snooping on his phone. Bettina likewise told Jahmar that Celeste was jealous because she didn't like being second choice. And informed him it was no secret with the crew that Vlad only ever went out with Celeste because Bettina herself had said no. Both denied all knowledge of the FFFC being anything other than a fantasy football league.'

Agnes dropped onto the floor and in her pyjamas and dressing gown recounted the awful confrontation with Tony. But she was too ashamed to mention the physical side of it. 'So now he knows what the FFFC really is. I'm going to get everyone into so much trouble.'

'No, you won't.'

'How can you say that?' Agnes spluttered. 'We've got two guests furious. If they complain—'

'I hardly think they're likely to do that,' Maria calmly replied as she doodled her boyfriend's name encircled with hearts on a notepad. 'What are they going to say? I slept with a member of staff of my own free will and it was so terrible I kept going back for more?'

'Yes, but—'

'But nothing. It won't go any further. And even if it did, the FFFC included Teflon Rodriguez and we all know nothing sticks to him. He'll work himself up into a terrific rage at being accused, management will be terrified of losing him and the whole thing will be quietly forgotten.' Maria leaned back in her chair and grinned. 'Honestly, passengers aren't worth the hassle. Luckily, I won't have to deal with them any longer.'

Agnes sat chewing her fingernails. It made sense what Maria was saying, which offered some consolation. At least nobody was going to get into trouble because of her. She caught her friend's perceptive look. 'Why don't you tell me the real reason you're upset?'

'Tony thinks I've used him,' Agnes whispered, and the tears started again. 'He believes it was all a game. When it wasn't. I don't want him to hate himself. What if he goes back and marries Sasha because he thinks it's easier that way? To stick with what he knows.'

Maria slammed her palm on the table. 'Listen to me, girl, the man drags you into a corridor to scream out his own inadequacies. And let's not forget he's the one who's shagged someone behind his fiancée's back. It's not your fault the bloke fell in love with you. Whatever he does next is up to him.'

'But I'm responsible for altering how he sees his life. Don't you get it? It is my fault. He would never have behaved like that otherwise.' Agnes clung to her teddy for emotional support and didn't care how childish she looked.

Maria shrugged as if it was no big deal. 'So go and explain yourself to him, if it's that important.'

'Are you out of your mind? He hates me.' She wrapped her arms around her knees in an attempt at self-comfort. And after the events in the corridor, she couldn't be in his company. The change in him had been terrifying. 'No, it's better for both of us if I keep away.'

'In other words, you're going to be a coward?' Maria slowly stood and motioned Agnes to do likewise.

'You give the best hugs.' Agnes blew her nose and sighed. 'Now get out of here. One of us at least should be enjoying their final night.'

Chapter Thirty-One

Clouds blotted out the moon and the stars and only a few voices echoed in the cold, bleak darkness. Everyone else had plans. Everybody else was behaving like rational and decent human beings. He no longer fell into that camp.

Tony stood against the guardrail and stared into nothingness, which perfectly summed up his life. Nothing to look forward to and nothing worth looking back on. Somewhere, a door opened and with it came a brief burst of laughter. Okay, maybe he was being a tad overdramatic. He had his health, a job, a home, his family, and friends. And he was also head of a pride. All that counted for something. But then again it didn't. He was absolute scum.

His friends were celebrating their last night together, but he couldn't bear to be amongst them with their jovial banter. His forthcoming nuptials hung over him like an executioner's axe. He'd imagined a bright new happy future with Agnes instead of a safe, unfulfilling, and frankly miserable one with Sasha. And if he went back home and got married that's what he was heading for. But if he called it off, he'd end up with nobody. Alone with his cats.

And if he didn't have wedding jokes to contend with, it was the enquiring looks from Patrick who appeared to be the only one to notice his bloodshot eyes. He was having a hard enough time holding it together and at the first opportunity had slipped away. Luckily, Jahmar was back to being so loved-up that a riot could have broken out in the bar and he'd fail to notice. After confronting both Vlad and Bettina, he'd been satisfied with their explanations that the FFFC was nothing sinister. The two members had been both bemused and embarrassed at the notion they were part of a sleazy grab-and-grope-a-passenger tally. Tony didn't have the heart to tell Jahmar the truth. What would it accomplish? Sometimes innocence was bliss.

The wind picked up and insistently tugged at his sketchpad. He'd been kidded into believing he had talent by Agnes. Sure, Vlad had said the same thing, but they were both part of the FFFC. Both liars. Both ready to trick unsuspecting fools. But not anymore. All he had to do was let go and his drawings and college portfolio would be swallowed up in the turbulent waters below. And he could easily follow them, down to the depths because wasn't that what he deserved?

He'd stayed in the corridor for thirty minutes after Agnes fled, wallowing in self-pity and hatred but then the horrific realisation slammed into him like a tsunami. He'd lost control and turned into a monster. In those few minutes he hadn't known himself, but now he did. He wanted to climb out of his skin, cast it aside and say 'but that isn't me, I'm not like that'. But he was. What difference did it make if it had only lasted a few minutes. You could do unspeakable things in such a short space of time. He retched up what little dinner he'd managed to force down and dragged the sleeve of his coat across his mouth. He wanted to cleanse himself of self-loathing and disgust. How had he come to this? He'd always been level-headed. His emotions never peaked or troughed but remained steady. But he had evil inside, and it had exploded out of him. What if it happened again?

He retched again. Maybe if he was sick enough it would expel the wickedness within. He rested his head on the cool guardrail and breathed deeply. Images of Sasha, Jahmar and Agnes floated into his consciousness. He had passed judgement on all of them, lambasted them for shameful, thoughtless, inappropriate behaviour but theirs paled next to his. Had Sasha ever attacked him? Had Jahmar forced himself on Agnes? Had Agnes misled him about the short-term nature of their relationship? The answer to each was a resounding no. Of course they hadn't. Their behaviour was hardly exemplary but so what? He'd lectured them on common decency when he had none.

The water churned below him. It would only take a few moments to throw his laughable attempts at art over the side. And why not join them? Did he deserve to live? And despite their faults, he didn't deserve the affections of Sasha, Jahmar or Agnes. He withdrew his sketchpad and balanced it on the guardrail. Let fate decide. If it went, it went. He wouldn't reach out to save the meaningless drawings of a shameful nobody.

'I wouldn't do that if I was you.' He turned to find Patrick and Sebastian hand in hand. They looked so happy together that he couldn't hold his emotions back any longer. Sebastian quickly stepped forward and as the sketchpad teetered and slid over the edge, he lunged and grabbed it. Tony allowed himself to be steered to the same seat he and Agnes had sat on. For five minutes he cried in the arms of his friend before sitting upright.

'I'm sorry, guys,' Tony croaked. 'You don't need to deal with this. It's your last night together. Go and have fun.'

'We have many years ahead of us for that,' Sebastian replied and smiled at Patrick. 'Tonight, it's more important for us to provide you with solace.'

'And there's something we need to tell you.' Patrick patted him on the knee. 'Agnes never used you. She never submitted any FFFC points during your time together.'

And the black hole of despair opened and welcomed him in. If Patrick had ripped his heart out, it couldn't be any worse. She'd tried to explain but he hadn't listened. If only he had. But now there was never any chance of them being together. The bile surged upwards, and he rushed forwards to throw up. But his stomach was empty.

'I don't deserve to live.' He staggered back to the bench and collapsed. Hot tears streamed down his face. 'But I don't even have the guts to end it.'

Patrick eyed him warily. 'Listen, boy. Nothing is bad enough to kill yourself over.'

'You don't understand.' His shoulders shook with all-consuming self-loathing. 'I-I attacked an innocent Agnes. How do I live with myself after that?'

Sebastian straightened his glasses, casting confused glances at Patrick. 'What are you talking about? Maria left Agnes not half an hour ago in their cabin. They sat and chatted, and she certainly would've told us if her friend was hurt. All Agnes kept repeating was that it was her fault.'

Tony crumpled; all the fight was gone. 'Agnes didn't do anything wrong. But I did.'

'I think you'd better explain, son. Because we're at a total loss as to what's going on.'

He so wanted Patrick to make everything better. His soothing words had always washed away past worries, but not this time. Like a plastic takeaway tub, he'd be forever stained inside. Nothing could erase what he'd done.

'I'm going to tell you exactly what happened.' Tony spat out the words. 'So you can both hate me as much as I hate myself. And I'm hoping after that you'll do what I can't and throw me overboard.'

Chapter Thirty-Two

The alarm sounded. Agnes groaned and hit snooze. Three minutes later it went off again. She hit snooze. After the fourth rendition of a marching band exploding inside the cabin, there was a string of French expletives from the bunk below and an abrupt instruction to get her bony backside out of bed, or else. Agnes sat up so fast she smacked her head on the ceiling, emitting swear words in her own native tongue.

'What the hell are you doing down there?' Agnes leaned over the bunk to find what appeared to be a small dormouse snuggled in a blanket.

'You didn't seriously think I was going to leave you alone last night, did you?' The huge brown eyes peered out. 'I crept back after bidding my lover au revoir. You were fast asleep with your teddy bear and looked so cute I took a photo.' Maria held it up for inspection and Agnes lobbed the teddy at Maria's head, who shot for cover, cackling with laughter.

It was her final shift of the cruise. The passengers would disembark after breakfast which luckily meant she wouldn't bump into Tony again. Agnes grimaced as she stared at her reflection in the ensuite mirror. She looked appalling, with dark bags under bloodshot eyes, but there was nothing for it. Work called. After bidding Maria farewell, she traipsed along the corridor, dragged her feet up the stairs, heaved open the door to be confronted with Tony (whose appearance echoed hers) and Patrick. She backed up, desperately fumbling for the door handle behind her.

'It's okay. I insisted Patrick joined me because I knew you'd be terrified if I turned up alone.' His tone was desperate and heartbroken. 'Sebastian and him know everything that happened in the corridor. I didn't sugarcoat anything, and I'm only amazed they didn't toss me over the side last night. I'm not here to cause trouble. I've come to apologise.' He glanced at his watch. 'It's almost time for you to start work, so I'll get right to the point. I know you withdrew from the FFFC, and I know you didn't sleep with me for the points.'

She smiled sadly at Patrick. 'It's okay, you don't have to stay. I know Tony won't do anything to scare me. Go and enjoy what little time you have left with Sebastian.'

'Bless you, my child. Good luck. I believe you'll achieve everything you deserve.' He blew her a kiss and she mimed catching it. And then he was gone.

It was only the two of them in what amounted to a glorified corridor. 'How did you find out?'

He returned a sad smile. 'You have your friend Maria to thank, again. She tracked down Sebastian last night and told him about submitting the points on your behalf and in turn he and Patrick told me. I'm so sorry for yesterday. I'm so sorry for everything.' His croaky voice wavered, and he raked his fingers down his face. 'I wish with all my heart I could take back the events of last night. I want to scream and shout at the person I was. To make them stop and listen to you. But I can't and I'm going to have to live with that for the rest of my pitiful life. I don't want to be me anymore. But what's the alternative?'

She stared horrified at the man before her. 'You can't kill yourself.'

'If I thought it'd help …' She blanched and he shook his head sadly. 'I wouldn't, it'd destroy my family and be utterly stupid and selfish. I repeated that I don't know how many times to Sebastian and Patrick last night, but despite my protests they wouldn't leave my side. I don't suppose babysitting a monster on their last night was any fun for them. Although you'll be glad to hear they quite rightly tore strips off me for my actions towards you.'

His voice held no hope and Agnes realised she'd never heard utter wretchedness till then. It came as no surprise to her that both men had kept a close watch on him. And gave her a kernel of satisfaction that both had also held him to account. Losing her father had resulted in rage, splitting up with her ex brought heartbreak, events in the corridor were terrifying but she'd never ever contemplated quitting. Life was tough sometimes, but you pushed through. How else did you succeed.

How else did you win?

She motioned him to follow her. 'Come on. I've got a little time to spare.'

A few minutes later they were on the top deck overlooking a pre-dawn Valletta. So much had happened in the last fortnight. She pointed to the quayside. 'That's where I first saw you.'

He stared down at the empty gangway that was ready to take all the passengers back to their everyday lives. He gripped the guardrail and dropped his head. 'I brought it all on myself, didn't I?' She stood silently, unsure what to say. 'Please forgive me.'

Fresh tears tracked down his unshaven face, a man at his lowest ebb. The events of the last two weeks played in her mind. Tony slapping Maria's backside, sitting terrified on the stallion, chatting on the top deck, praising his drawings, confiding in one another, the salsa class, a magical night of luxury and passion, him staggering drunk around her cabin professing undying love. The scene changed and she was on her knees in the corridor, begging him, shouting at him and then cowering in her cabin. And now they were standing side by side, each frightened and full of regrets. She had it in her power to help or hinder him. To offer a lifeline or slam the door in his face. Which one was it to be?

'I forgive you.' His shoulders relaxed but before he could respond she held up her hand as a warning. 'But what you did to me must never happen again. I never want anyone else to go through that. It was absolutely terrifying and because of that you must never forget.'

She certainly wouldn't … his twisted face and the chilling change in him. To be confronted by somebody out of control, who couldn't be reasoned with, was seared into her memory and she'd never put herself in that position again. And all because he thought she was playing a game.

He clutched his heart, as if checking it was still there. 'On my life, I promise never to forget, and to never do anything like that again.'

Agnes shivered in her uniform. The air was cool, and the first traces of light appeared on the horizon. But the coldness came from within. 'I shouldn't have played the game.' There, she'd said it, and with it came relief. She wasn't responsible for Tony's actions, but she hadn't been entirely blameless either.

He frowned. 'You didn't play the game with me though.'

'But I did with others, who were oblivious to the fact. I thought it was a bit of fun. What harm could it possibly do?' She shivered again at the memories of the FFFC sitting together and laughing at their foolhardy passengers. She was sickened and disgusted with herself and seriously needed to reset her moral compass. He'd lost control. Mild-mannered Tony, the last person you'd ever expect. And it drove home to her that anyone was capable of violence. All it took was a trigger, and she'd been Tony's. Hadn't Rodriguez warned her of the dangers in breaking somebody's heart. What was her trigger? Agnes hoped never to find out. And above all she was sorry for making him love her. But she didn't say any of that and instead gave him a tight smile. 'I'm sorry I changed how you saw your life. For making you realise you weren't happy.'

He laughed a clear and joyous sound that reached inside her and helped to dislodge some of the sadness. 'You encouraged me to follow my dreams and you told me you weren't the answer. And in both cases, you were right. I need to find my own way and to do that I need to be myself.'

They leaned over the guardrail together and watched the city stir into action. How many of those in the warren of streets were saying their goodbyes to each other? Or how many were waking up with their true love?

'I'm glad to hear that.' She turned to face him. 'So, what are you going to do?'

'Well for starters, I'm definitely not getting married. That would be the biggest mistake of my life. We'd be divorced within a year or become one of those couples who stay together while hating each other's guts. Life's too short for that.'

'You're too good for her,' she replied forcefully. 'I can't believe it took you so long to realise. Imagine if you'd never come on this cruise. You'd have ended up marrying her.'

He shuddered. 'That's exactly what my mum and sisters said when I told them last night.'

'Wow, you've actually started telling people.'

He laughed again. 'Oh yes. I was consumed by so much self-loathing last night I thought why not pile more on. Patrick and Sebastian counselled me to wait till I got home but I wanted to act. After I chatted to my family, I rang Sasha and broke the news.'

Instinctively she went to grab his arm but stopped short. She couldn't do it and let her hand drop to her side. It didn't go unnoticed, and he quickly looked away. 'What did she say? What did she do?' Images of an irate women ripping a house to pieces sprung to mind. Agnes couldn't imagine Princess Sasha taking the news of being dumped well. Imagine having to notify all those people that the wedding was off.

He nodded as if reading her mind. 'It was rather amusing. At first, she laughed and told me to ring back when I was sober and in my right mind. When I said no, I meant every word, I hadn't been drinking and we wouldn't be getting married because neither of us could make the other happy, she hung up on me. I wasn't quite sure what to do next but then my phone rang, and it was Jahmar demanding to know what was going on—'

'That must have been an interesting conversation?'

'I don't think I'm in Celeste's good books today by ruining her last night with Jahmar. At first, he ordered me back to our room. I promptly told him to shove it and if he wanted to talk, he'd have to come to Patrick's room to see me.'

Agnes clapped her hands in admiration. 'Check you out, Mr I Won't Take Any Crap Off Anyone Anymore. And did he?'

'Oh yes, he arrived within five minutes and was livid, threatening me with all sorts. Patrick and Sebastian went and stood in the corridor to give us some privacy but said they'd be back in if Jahmar so much as threatened a hair on my head – which was equally amusing as they'd threatened to rip my head off after I told them everything. I sat him down and explained that the cruise had made me realise I wasn't the man to make his sister happy. I said I'd pay back the cruise and understood if he didn't want to see me anymore.'

'And how did he take it?'

He grimaced and avoided eye contact. 'Well, remember I was a total mess. It was obvious to Jahmar that I'd been sobbing my heart out. And I sort of … well, I let him believe I was utterly distraught because I was breaking up with his sister.'

She slowly grinned. 'You sly dog.'

'It seemed the best course of action. Jahmar is none the wiser about the FFFC or us and much to my amazement he said the breakup might be the shock his sister needs.' He scratched his stubble and frowned. 'Neither of us believe that though. Anyway, he broke the news to her when I was sitting there. Oh my God you should have heard her. She threatened to kill me, shred my clothes, torch my car, change the locks so I couldn't get in my own house. In the end Jahmar told her to shut up. He'd ring their parents who'd come and pick her up. And that's exactly what he did.'

She knew it was cruel, but a giggle started to bubble up at the vision of Sasha being led out of the house by her indignant parents. And once she started laughing, she couldn't stop. Tony joined in and soon tears were running down their faces.

'But aren't you worried she'll come back today and go on a rampage? I mean what's stopping her?'

'In I way I hope she does.' Agnes frowned and he gave a mischievous grin. 'My eldest sister has taken up residence till I get back. Sasha never had any time for my family, who've always kept quiet because of me. But now—'

'But now you're no longer a couple, they can let rip.'

'Lori's exact words were "well it won't take that waste of space long to pack, she never paid for a goddam thing in the house". It'll make for an interesting meeting I think.'

'And what about your art class?' Agnes crossed her fingers and prayed he wouldn't give up on his dream.

'I'll develop my portfolio, attend a local art club and take some online courses until I can properly start next year. That way, I can work plenty of overtime as a safety net and I've decided to study part-time as it makes more sense.' Previously she would have given him a hug but now she merely nodded. He fumbled in his rucksack and extracted a cardboard tube. 'This is for you. It's an apology, although it can't make up for what I did. Think of it as a good luck memento.'

She carefully unrolled it with shaking hands. It was a beautiful sketch of her standing on the top deck looking out to Corfu Town. A golf ball had taken up residency in her throat, making it hard to talk. 'It-it's gorgeous. You're so talented … put the work in and you'll succeed.'

The smile was shy this time and he self-consciously pointed to the bottom right-hand corner where there was a swirly Anthony Acebi and a smiley face. 'If I become famous, that'll be worth a fortune.'

She nodded. 'I'm counting on it. This is my nest egg.'

They still stood apart, but the space had narrowed to a sliver. Would either one bridge the divide? Yesterday's confrontation lingered, changing the dynamics. They could stand facing Valletta and chat, but eye contact was minimal and there was no touching. The bond was broken. Neither spoke as the sky continued to lighten.

'Take care, Agnes. You're a remarkable woman.' His words tripped over themselves. The clock was counting down. They turned at last to face one another. His face was pained, and he smiled sadly. 'There's one lucky man out there who's going to steal your heart. I'm only sorry it wasn't me.'

And then he crossed the divide and with a quick peck on her cheek he turned and fled.

'Tony, I'm—'

But he was gone and as Agnes studied the drawing, she figured it was just as well he'd kept going because what more was there to say?

Chapter Thirty-Three

They were all back in the opulent Mariners cocktail lounge. Past and present members of the FFFC gathered for the end of season prize giving, and again fake piano music tinkled in the background for non-existent guests. The passengers were all gone and in her mind's eye, Agnes pictured Tony at the airport. Would he be fielding questions from his mates who now knew the wedding was off? Or would they all be getting lashed, determined to retain the holiday vibe until the plane's wheels touched down at Heathrow? She'd never know, and a sadness settled over her once more. Even the FFFC were unusually sombre.

Tomas stood and raised a glass. Dressed in his officer's whites, it wasn't difficult to see why members of all sexes swooned over the handsome Italian. 'As the newly elected chairman of the FFFC it gives me great pleasure to present Maria with this season's trophy.'

There was a round of applause, accompanied by cheers from some and pantomime boos from a resplendent Rodriguez in a tuxedo jacket, crisp white shirt and full-length taffeta skirt. Agnes joined in but her heart wasn't in it. The sooner the ceremony ended, the better.

'Thank you, thank you.' Maria held the diminutive trophy aloft. 'I couldn't have done it all without the help of our passengers and the departure and bad luck of many of the FFFC members.'

Tomas tapped the side of his glass with a spoon and nodded at the remaining club members. 'With Sebastian, Rodriguez and Agnes withdrawing from the FFFC and Maria leaving us, those of us left have made the decision to disband the group.'

Vlad grasped Bettina's hand and gently kissed her three crushed fingers. 'We need to grow up and start acting our age.'

Maria raised her eyebrow. 'Are we to believe that the two of you have finally given in to the obvious truth that you are besotted with one another?'

The pair gave shy smiles and nodded.

Rodriguez snorted and gave Vlad a withering look. 'For someone who purports to be intelligent, you can be incredibly dense.' Vlad frowned as Rodriguez sipped his champagne. 'All you ever needed to do was quit the FFFC for Bettina to agree to go out with you.'

Vlad's face was such a picture of incredulity that everyone laughed.

'Is that right, Ti? Is that all I needed to do?' His girlfriend smiled and nodded. 'But … but w-why didn't you tell me that? I'd have quit ages ago. It's only ever been you.'

She lovingly stroked his face. 'You really do have so much to learn.'

'Women never tell you what they want, son.' Sebastian smiled and winked at Bettina. 'Always be afraid of a female who states she's *fine* when you ask if everything's okay. Because she certainly isn't.'

Vlad and Tomas both looked utterly perplexed and shook their heads at one another as if to say women were unfathomable.

'Love certainly seems to be in the air,' Agnes added. 'Vlad and Bettina, Maria and lover boy and what about you, Sebastian? What's happening with your budding romance?'

A slow smile spread across his slim face. 'I'll continue aboard for now. Patrick works away so we're going to figure out the best plan with our rotas. But the intention will be for us to set up home somewhere in the not-too-distant future.'

Rodriguez raised his champagne flute. 'I think I speak for us all when I say it couldn't have happened to a better person. And on a personal note, I'm immensely happy that you've found love at last. I'm only sorry I played my part in it taking so long.'

'Thank you, Roddy. That means the world to me.' Sebastian stood and the men shook hands.

'Wow, does this mean you're actually going to be nice to one another?' Maria asked and the pair nodded. 'Typical, you wait until I'm leaving to bury the hatchet.' But she gave a pixie grin.

'Did you know Celeste is also leaving?' Vlad said and most of them shook their heads. 'She came to bid me farewell, stating life on board wasn't for her and she was off to start a new life with her multi-millionaire boyfriend.'

'She also came to gloat.' Bettina smirked. 'I told her if she was happy with being second choice, good for her.'

'I guess you'll not be getting an invite to their wedding?' Maria added and frowned. 'I thought she might have at least told me. I guess I won't be going either.'

At the mention of weddings, Agnes blushed but luckily nobody noticed. She wondered what lay in store for Tony when he returned home. Would Sasha dig her heels in or swiftly move on? It would probably be the latter. Would Tony remember his brief holiday romance, or would he be too busy with his new life? For better or worse, Agnes understood that her fling with Tony had fundamentally changed her. It had altered how she saw herself, how her actions could have unexpected and sometimes dire repercussions … because if you pushed somebody too far, they were capable of anything. The memory of her dalliance would forever remain with her and maybe with Tony too.

Everyone raised their glasses. 'To new beginnings.'

Agnes glanced at Rodriguez, who gave her a wink and she coughed nervously. 'I won't be here next season either. I'm transferring to another ship.'

There was a collective cry of woe and calls for her to reconsider, but she shook her head. It was time to move on.

Rodriguez slammed his glass down on the table. 'Good grief, am I the only person on this ship capable of entertaining people with a good story?' He narrowed his eyes at Agnes, who shook her head. 'Fine, I'll tell them. Our rising star summoned up all her courage and went to see her idol. Louis.'

'You can't call him that. It's Monsieur Baffier,' Agnes spluttered.

He ignored her and continued. 'She handed Louis the job application and asked if he would be a reference. And do you know what he did?' Everyone shook their heads. 'He flicked through all the vacancies, folded his arms and said no.'

Bettina clutched Agnes's arm. 'Oh my God, what did you do?'

'I wanted the ground to open up and swallow me whole,' Agnes responded and winced at the memory. 'I muttered my apologies for wasting his time and turned to crawl into some dark corner and die of embarrassment.'

'But tell them what happened next?' Rodriguez butted in excitedly. He was clearly loving the retelling, a born entertainer.

'Monsieur Baffier called me back and pointed to another vacancy and said that was the one I should go for. But it was way beyond me, and I flat out stated I couldn't do it. He said it would be unbelievably difficult, it would stretch me to breaking point, but he had utter faith I could do it. So, I reluctantly nodded as I was in shock.'

'Wow,' Vlad chimed in. 'That's totally amazing.'

Rodriguez laughed. 'That's not even the best bit. Louis promptly picks up the phone, telling Agnes he knows the chef so he's going to ring her up. And do you know what Agnes did?'

Again, everyone shook their heads and he motioned for Agnes to take up the story.

'I told him he couldn't do that. There were rules and regulations to follow. You couldn't just ring the chef and leapfrog everyone.'

'My God, you really are an idiot at times,' Tomas interrupted.

'How many brain cells do you have rattling around in your skull?' Vlad said, rolling his eyes at a smirking Bettina.

'Okay, okay I get the point.' Agnes held up her hands.

Sebastian cast his gaze over the group. 'Agnes has integrity. It would do well for some of you to remember that.'

She smiled at the muttered apologies. 'Monsieur Baffier said if I had a three-star Michelin chef in my corner it would be wise to shut up.'

She had indeed kept quiet and let him get on with it. The call connected and through the speaker came an abrupt Asian female voice. The chefs exchanged pleasantries which involved railing against the declining standards in culinary expertise. Both ranted about famous chefs who were happy to live off past glories and had never done anything in years to justify their exorbitant fees. Agnes had clamped her hand over her mouth, so her laughter didn't sneak out.

After a few minutes of putting the world to rights, Monsieur Baffier had informed the scary voice that her search for a chef was over as he had the ideal candidate. To which the voice had laughed and said she'd thought it was high time he'd found his next prodigy. Light-hearted banter went back and forth, enough for Agnes to work out that the voice had been a former Baffier apprentice. And then the next thing, Agnes was being grilled. For thirty minutes she was bombarded with increasingly difficult questions and by the end her armpits were damp with sweat. The two chefs chatted a bit further and the aggressive voice asked if her former teacher was willing to bet his reputation on Agnes. He snapped of course he was, why would he have rung otherwise. And in under an hour Agnes found herself with a new job.

'When do you start?' Bettina asked.

'Next week,' Agnes replied. It was an unbelievably fast turnaround. She had to be in Los Angeles in three days' time and would have a few days familiarisation before embarking on an eleven-week Pacific Odyssey cruise. It was both terrifying and exhilarating.

'You're hardcore, girl.' Maria shook her head in admiration. She'd been the first person Agnes told and had been rewarded with a massive hug.

'To whatever comes next.' Agnes raised her glass, and everyone did the same. It was time to move on and she couldn't wait to get started.

Epilogue

Three years later.

The on-board kitchen was a well-oiled machine. Agnes swept her eagle eyes appreciatively across the tidy benches. The team had, as always, done a fantastic job. There'd been the usual congratulations from the head maître d', and tonight the captain had popped in to pass on his, the crew and passengers' compliments. They weren't even halfway through their Caribbean cruise, so the visit was unexpected but always appreciated.

Ahmad accompanied her up the warmly lit corridor. Everything about this cruise ship was understated luxury. 'Will you be joining us for drinks, tonight?' And as usual, she declined with the standard response of having too much to do. Usually, her friend (her only friend on board) would nod, but tonight was different. He halted their progress with insistent pressure to her arm and she begrudgingly stopped and leaned against a decorative wall panel.

'How long have we worked together?' It was a question he knew the answer to, so she kept quiet. He crossed his arms and maintained eye contact. 'It's been one year and one day. Seven months on the last ship and five months one day on this one. And in all that time, how often have you joined the team get-togethers?' Again, he knew the answer but this time the tall, rail-thin chef from the Punjab refused to break the silence and she was forced to.

'I never have.' She shifted her weight from one hip to the other, crossed her arms and scowled. 'And your point is?'

'It's not healthy to lock yourself away each night. You eat alone, you don't talk to anyone except at work and rarely leave the ship. It's not right. I'm worried about you.' His tone as ever was calm and measured. In stature and temperament, he reminded her strongly of Sebastian. They even wore the same wire-framed glasses. Agnes was under no illusion that the team operated so efficiently because of him. His people management was phenomenal, surpassed only by his skills as a chef. There was no doubt about it, the man was a genius. Agnes was good. She knew that and as proof had risen through the ranks to reach Head Chef in less than two years. Her skill was in creating mouth-watering dishes in an array of different cuisines and she was passionate about expanding her knowledge to introduce new ingredients and dishes showcasing different cultures. However, Ahmad was in another league entirely. He had the vision to mix different cuisines into fantastic fusion dishes. He'd been headhunted for his latest role but had refused the position unless it included Agnes. She was flattered by how highly he rated her, and they made a perfect team. He called her his secret weapon, a rough diamond who held everyone in check. Others had less kind nicknames. She knew a few of them – *the wicked witch*, *vulture face* and *hard heartless bitch* to name a few. The latter was often screamed in her face when she had to give staff their marching orders. She let the name-calling wash over her, but it hadn't always been that way. She'd toughened up since those early days on the Pacific Odyssey cruise and she had her former boss Miss Huang to thank.

Three years ago, Agnes had arrived in Los Angeles to board a smaller and more luxurious cruise ship than the Mediterranean one. There were less than a thousand passengers but what the ship lacked in numbers it made up for in its superior standards, especially the food. Her induction had been a total immersion into the company's culture and fantastically high standards. And nobody's standards came higher than those of her new boss – Miss Huang. She was in her early forties, elegant, impeccable and a firecracker. Agnes quickly learned never to refer to her as a top female chef or top female anything for that matter as it unleashed a tirade. She would storm around the kitchen pointing at her nether regions shouting why was it that owning a vagina had to be dragged into everything? Why was it always top female this, top female that? When did you ever see a list of top male chefs, the next male chefs to look out for? Never. It didn't happen. Miss Huang wanted to be known as a top chef or *the* top chef. There should be no gender separation because why did it make any difference whether you had a vagina, a penis or anything else for that matter. What mattered was that exceptional cuisine was served for their paying guests. End of. It had taken a few weeks for Agnes to get used to these outbursts, and then it became part of the everyday noise of working in a pressure cooker.

She'd known the role would make or break her, and intended it to be the former. Monsieur Baffier had been right. It stretched her beyond anything she'd ever done or hoped for. She made herself a sponge to soak up every droplet of knowledge. But almost a year in, Agnes had wobbled when a decidedly nasty, disgruntled, and junior colleague with delusions of grandeur and ability screamed at her for another colleague's oversight. He'd railed at being victimised and discriminated because he had testicles, said he'd been passed over for promotion yet again (Agnes got the job) because he didn't have breasts. She'd stood her ground in the face of a vicious onslaught including her alleged mistakes, her inferior abilities and lack of people skills. She'd put him right, firmly and calmly, but it severely shook her. Later, Miss Huang had pulled her to one side and had given her an important lesson. The higher you rose, the more people hated and envied you. The only way to succeed was to harden up and not put a step wrong. She'd then given Agnes the task of sacking the gentleman in question for gross insubordination and failing to reach the minimum standards expected. He was the first one to shriek 'heartless bitch' into her face. She'd carefully wiped the spittle off her cheek and given him fifteen minutes to pack his bags or security would escort him ashore. The experience was awful, but it had to be done. There'd been others, and with each one it added another scale to her armour-plated exterior.

For over two years, Agnes had worked under Miss Huang to blossom and attain her Head Chef goal. But then Ahmad joined, and she instantly saw his superior talent. It could have gone one of two ways. They could have become bitter rivals, locked in a battle of one-upmanship. But Agnes was no fool. Like Monsieur Baffier and Miss Huang, she knew Ahmad Yadhav could raise her game again and, unbeknown to her, she did the same for him. They hit it off instantly and constantly conferred and compared their ideas with one another. As a pair, they pushed and encouraged one another, both obsessed with food and what you could do with it. And in turn the kitchen produced outstanding results. People talked, news spread, praise flooded in, Miss Huang and the management were delighted. But then Ahmad was headhunted for his dream job, but he refused to go without her. He said they were opposite sides of a bank note and if you took away one, all value was lost. The gold-plated opportunity had to be grasped but despite that, telling Miss Huang was one of the hardest things Agnes had ever done. But in the end, it worked out perfectly. Miss Huang wished them good luck with a wink. A month later, she'd jumped ship to set up a restaurant in Tokyo.

But now, months later, in the best job she'd ever had, Agnes stood and eyeballed Ahmad. He was the good cop to her bad cop (or more accurately, brooding, intense, solitary cop). And that role suited her perfectly, thank you very much. She kept everyone at arm's length, and maintained a healthy distance (regardless of what Ahmad said) from colleagues. She refused to let anyone get close. Ahmad was the exception but their friendship (there was no physical attraction on either side, and never had been) was based purely on a culinary obsession to create the best dishes.

Agnes hadn't had a sexual encounter since Tony, and refused to dwell on her lack of intimacy with others. There wasn't time for such frivolous notions. Did she miss sex? Did it matter? But she'd been right – the brief interlude with Tony continued to deeply affect her. In the confines of a kitchen, she was confident and highly competent. It was her safe space she adored. But away from the heat, the aromas and the deadlines, she struggled and no longer trusted herself around others. She was a trigger, a flint, a vessel that had transformed a seemingly level-headed individual into a monster. She refused to put herself in a position to do so again. In a nutshell, she didn't like herself much, so didn't expect anyone else to either. And as a result, she'd drifted away from friends and rarely spoke to her family. They knew she worked hard and were proud.

At least the encounter with Tony had mellowed her attitude towards her father. She realised he was only human; he'd made a stupid mistake that cost him his life, but she could forgive him. Even so, she only sent the odd text, email, and rang on special occasions (if she had the time) but she'd never been home for years and as time passed, she realised she probably never would. As long as her family were happy and healthy that was all that mattered. And they were. She was kept abreast of the Karapetsa clan by her youngest brother who refused to be fobbed off by her lack of communication. He messaged her every week and booked himself onto her cruises so he could drag her almost kicking and screaming from the confines of her cabin. She loved (and hated) him for that.

Ahmad was watching her closely. He reminded her of an owl. A wise beyond his years owl. She often forgot they were the same age.

'I'm fine, there's no need to worry.' She rubbed tired eyes. 'I think I'll get an early night.'

He sighed but as always nodded. 'I'm not the only one who's worried about you – so's Viktor.'

Viktor Benrubi. Even his name sent a delicious shiver up her spine. Something Ahmad knew fine well, and it was the whole reason he'd mentioned the talented pastry chef's name.

The day she walked into the kitchen and saw him standing there, her heart rate accelerated, like a Formula One car blasting off the grid. It was impossible to miss him. Broad, muscular, six-foot-seven and ruggedly handsome with dishevelled jet-black hair. His face told a story without him having to say a word. A nose broken more than once and a long thin white scar on his left cheek. And when he spoke, she'd melted into a puddle on the floor. It was a deep, resonant and unbelievably sexy voice. When he'd embraced Ahmad it was like watching a grizzly bear grasp an upright sapling in the forest. Ever since they'd worked together, Ahmad had been on a mission to entice the man-mountain to join him. It had taken him almost four years. Viktor was exceptional and Ahmad wanted the best people around him – because, like ingredients, he said if you didn't have the very best it didn't matter what you did, you'd never produce truly amazing results.

After releasing Ahmad, Viktor had stuck out his hand to Agnes and said he was excited to be working with such a talented chef, she was all Ahmad talked about. When their hands touched, electricity surged through every nerve ending. The connection was so intense she'd expected scorch marks on her fingertips, and she'd dissolved into a star-struck teenager who could barely manage to string two words together.

The extreme reaction terrified her. But, even so, once alone with Ahmad, she grilled him for every detail about her devilishly handsome colleague. Infuriatingly, he'd calmly responded that he wasn't going to be a go-between. If she fancied him, she was going to have to crawl out of her hermit shell, pull on her big girl pants and talk to him herself. She'd spluttered indignantly at the ludicrous notion that she was in any way attracted to his friend. How could he have such a ridiculous idea? But all he did was smirk. It forced Agnes to eavesdrop at every opportunity, to gradually built up a picture of her fellow Greek. He'd grown up in Thessaloniki where his family ran a successful bakery chain but, aged twenty-one, he'd opted for life at sea. Viktor kept the kitchen entertained with amusing anecdotes about growing up in a baking-obsessed family and his time spent on various cruise ships.

In a matter of weeks, he was a firm favourite with the team. It wasn't only his presence that demanded attention, there was more to him than that. Agnes was a literal person, she believed in what she could touch, taste, hear and see. She didn't believe in ghosts, an afterlife, crystals, ley lines or countless other things which she lumped into touchy-feely crap. However, all of that counted for nothing with Viktor. He had an aura. It shimmered, and, in his presence, an overwhelming sense of calmness wrapped itself around her. And she wasn't the only one to notice. Frazzled colleagues would sidle up to him for a hit of tranquillity and it became part of kitchen life. Some just needed to stand near him, others briefly touched his arm, while a particularly forward young lady always requested a hug to calm fraught nerves. Agnes narrowed her eyes and breathed deeply every time that happened, while in her mind's eye she launched a potato at the Egyptian's forehead. The first time, Viktor had caught her. She'd quickly looked away, face burning. He'd smiled, with a twinkle in his eye as if he knew her violent thoughts. And from that point on she'd shut him down completely if he attempted any small talk. They conversed purely about work, and he was another reason not to attend any social gatherings.

Agnes didn't trust herself in his company. Her reactions and emotions operated with no regards to reason, intellect or common sense. A fortnight earlier, she'd been finalising the menu with Ahmad. They'd been sitting in the office, drinking coffee when he casually mentioned that Viktor was dating one of the waitresses. A desperate wail escaped her lips. The espresso cup skittered across the table and smashed on the floor. And then he'd started to laugh and said he was only joking. Agnes had gripped the table for fear she might frisbee her saucer at his smug face. But she'd never been so relieved to discover Viktor was still single. But for how long? The man was a catch. No, he was *the* catch.

***

The night breeze tickled her arms as she sat tucked up on a lounger in a hidden corner of the deck. Her secret spot where night after night she came to unwind in the safety of the darkness because there was no longer any early morning drawing. That passion had been extinguished when she said goodbye to Tony.

It was late and the ship sailed towards another postcard-perfect Caribbean island. Tomorrow morning, the passengers would disembark to photograph yet more palm trees and white sandy beaches, trek into the interior, scuba dive in the lagoon or sit and sip cocktails at one of the harbourside bars. But at this ungodly hour, they were tucked up in bed. Footsteps approached and she tensed. Nobody was ever out at this time, and she hoped they'd continue by.

'Hello, there.' That caramel-coated voice slid into her ears and wrapped itself around her heart. She glanced up slowly, attempting to calm the thumping in her chest. She wouldn't be surprised if he could hear it from where he stood not five metres away, dressed in loose trousers and a hoodie with 'USA' emblazoned across the front. 'Do you mind if I join you?' He was already drawing up another chair. How presumptuous could you get? 'I'm having trouble sleeping and thought the fresh air might do me some good.'

She could hardly refuse him so nodded, and he sat down within touching distance. Her fingers twitched and she angrily overrode her body's desire to reach out and hold his hand. He glanced down and she caught the faintest smile around his beautiful lips, but he didn't say a word and neither did she. The comfortable silence stretched out. She closed her eyes and listened to his breathing mixed with the gentle hum of the engines.

'Agnes, please. Can you just be quiet for five minutes? I mean, it's non-stop.'

She turned her head and he grinned. A slow, sexy grin. She wanted to rip his clothes off, right there and then. But instead, she scowled. 'I said you could join me. I didn't say I was happy to have a conversation with you.'

'Excuse me.' He scratched his scar. 'I think you'll find you didn't say anything at all. There was the slightest inclination of your head, as if it was far too much effort to form a sentence. Do you only have an allotted number of words to use each day and you're running low?'

He was humouring her, but she refused to take the bait and instead drew a blanket around her shoulders and settled back into the chair.

'Come on, Agnes. Ask me a question. Anything you like. And I promise to answer.'

How could anybody refuse an offer like that? She shuffled to face him and hoped to sound supremely uninterested. 'Okay then, how did you break your nose and how did you get that scar?'

'Well, we've run into a little problem there, haven't we. You've asked me two questions instead of one. What to do?' He tapped his chin, and she heard the laughter behind his words. He was having far too much fun on her account. She gave him her best sly eyes, but he merely shrugged. 'I can only answer one, which is it to be?'

She sighed dramatically and grasped the blanket tightly. 'Fine, have it your way. The nose. How did you break your nose?'

He rubbed his hands gleefully and her irritation at him easily scoring points increased. 'I was hoping you'd pick that one as it's the better story. We can gloss over the first time – I was drunk and after stumbling out of bed to find the bathroom, I walked straight into a wall.' She sniggered and he raised an eyebrow. 'Charming. Anyway, the second time a passenger smacked me in the face with a fire extinguisher after I bedded his wife.' She sat bolt upright. He'd captured her attention now and she demanded to know why he'd done such a terrible thing.

It had been for a bet. Five years earlier, he'd worked on a huge cruise liner, nothing like their current compact one. He'd been cocky back then, an arrogant git to be precise and incredibly bored with a job he could do standing on his head. Not a good combination. He always got plenty of female attention, but it was all a bit too easy, so when he was invited to join a certain club, he leapt at the chance. Agnes shifted uneasily in her chair, but he didn't seem to notice and continued. The name of the game was to seduce somebody on board. You didn't get to pick who it was but instead you were allotted an individual by a teammate. Viktor was given a mid-thirties, mousey, nothing-to-write-home-about wife and mother of two teenage sons who were all holidaying together. A typical family, doing typical things on a standard cruise. All pretty humdrum, so he thought it'd be easy. A bit of flirting and after a day or so she'd drop her knickers for him. Job done and he'd undoubtedly have time to conquer a second punter to earn extra points. Agnes sucked in her breath; the sheer nerve of the guy was galling.

However, Mrs Everyday proved a surprisingly difficult nut to crack, and it took almost the full two weeks to break her down. But on the penultimate night, he'd succeeded. The poor thing had genuinely believed they were going to set up a new life together and after he'd laughed in her face, she'd fled in tears.

The next day, the husband confronted him after his wife for reasons unknown had come clean about a rather enjoyable tussle in the sack. It broke the guy's heart and destroyed their marriage. So, in revenge, he'd lain in wait for Viktor and then swung a fire extinguisher full force and knocked him out cold. The whole episode turned into a total nightmare for everyone involved. Luckily, or unluckily, depending on whose shoes you were in, the ship was sailing in international waters and the complicated nature of maritime law eventually saw the husband bought off with a free cruise.

'I still remember the anguished look on the man's face,' Viktor mumbled. He slumped forward with elbows on his knees, all bravado gone. His face was etched with pain. 'The guy said he hoped I was happy with what I'd done and then it all went black.'

Agnes pulled her knees up to her chest. 'Because that's when you were hit in the face?'

He nodded and edged his seat closer to hers. Their knees touched and again that jolt of electricity coursed through her blood. 'It wasn't my finest hour and as you can imagine it's not a story I wish to broadcast.'

Despite the overwhelming urge to launch herself at him she stared out to sea. Something wasn't right. She couldn't reconcile the story with the man sitting beside her. Admittedly, she hardly knew him, but her instincts were screaming at her not to believe him. Something was wrong, very wrong and she took a deep breath because if it was a lie, why had he picked that particular one? 'Is that story even true?'

'Does it matter if it isn't?' She sat quietly for a moment, trying to work out what to say. 'By the way, Rodriguez says hi.'

'You know about the FFFC, don't you?' She wasn't angry at her former colleague, more relieved that Viktor knew, which came as a surprise.

'I know you've drifted away from your friend, but he keeps tabs on you.' Agnes was hit by shame at letting the friendship slide but incredibly touched that Rodriguez still cared. 'He knows you keep to your room and have built up a protective wall to be safe. He said it doesn't work and to remember the night of slippers, dressing gowns and pizza.'

She did remember that night, of how she saw him as a lonely, misunderstood soul. Was that what she'd become? 'Does Rodriguez still stick to his cabin?'

He wobbled his hand side to side. 'It's fifty-fifty now, which is better than when I first started working with him. We became good friends, and he was excited when I told him I'd be working with you. Don't live in the past, Agnes. You can't undo it. Forgive yourself and move on.'

'But what if I can't?' she whispered and curled up tighter. 'You weren't there. You didn't see what happened when somebody thought I'd tricked them. A switch flicked, they became a different person, and in those few seconds it was terrifying. And I made that happen.'

He gently took her hand. 'Are you afraid that's what you'll do to me? That you'll somehow push me beyond my limits, and I'll lose control?'

'Not just you, but anyone. What if I have something inside me that brings out the worst in people?' Ahmad called her his rough diamond. But she saw herself differently. She was diamond-tipped, designed to break through anything, given the right pressure.

He shook his head. 'I don't believe that any more than you do. I think you're scared to be loved, that's all. I think you've worked so hard to get to where you are that you think there isn't room for anything else.'

She went to deny it but stopped. Was that true? Her mentors Monsieur Baffier and Miss Huang had been single, they'd put their careers before everything else. Is that what you had to do to succeed, to be number one? Maybe. Professionally, she was where she wanted to be. But what came next? She could easily become cocooned in her cabin because it was safer than risking being rejected. She might not watch reruns but she was becoming reclusive.

'You're right, I am scared to be loved and I'm terrified that any relationship will harm my career. I've worked so hard to get to where I am that selfishly I don't want to jeopardise it for something that might not last.' There, she'd said it. Her fears were out in the open. Would he despise her for them, think her weak and self-centred? Best to find out now.

His eyes were boring into hers. He was searching her soul, and she was stripped bare. It was incredibly painful and arousing at the same time. She could be with this man and that was even more frightening than anything else.

'But what if it does last, Agnes? What if a relationship makes each person grow? What if they support one another, nurture one another and expand each other's horizons? We could do anything we put our minds to. Isn't it worth taking the chance? Isn't it worth taking that chance on me? On us?'

She inhaled, filling her lungs with warm salt-laden air, and then exhaled deeply. Viktor was right. She needed to stop running. And she wanted him. She'd known that the second she clapped eyes on him.

'Okay, Mr Benrubi, you've got yourself a deal.' She stuck out her hand and he laughed, a deep booming sound, and the hairs on the back of her neck stood up. He leaned over and kissed her on the cheek.

'Get some sleep, sweetheart.' He stood and he held out his hand, but she shook her head.

'I'm going to stay out a little bit longer.' But then a thought grabbed her. 'Can you dance?'

He straightened an imaginary tie. 'You're looking at Mr Line Dancing Extraordinaire. I can out-strut anyone.'

Heat radiated up her face at an image of him in cowboy boots and nothing else. 'Why don't you show me some of those moves tomorrow?'

Acknowledgements

From the very first draft of Apokeri Bay to its final version, I stripped out twenty thousand words! All that carefully crafted text ended up on the cutting room floor.

Well, not quite.

I figure if I've taken the time to write it all, I might as well squirrel it away. Who knows when it'll come in handy?

So why cut text out in the first place? Sometimes it's edited out because (truth be told) it's crap, or it slows the story, or it isn't relevant, or it takes the reader down a cul-de-sac. And sometimes it's too early in the story for a character to blurt out their inner most secrets.

And the latter, led to Agnes Karapetsa is All at Sea.

I spent quite a bit of time writing a chunk of text where a group of Apokeri Bay characters have a confessional conflab. But it just didn't sit right in the novel. The characters at that point, didn't know each other well enough. However, Agnes's story lodged in my brain and took root. And what started out as a short back story to be included in my newsletter, morphed into a novella of almost fifty thousand words!

I do hope you enjoy this glimpse into Agnes's life pre-Apokeri Bay.

As always, I am eternally grateful for the unwavering support of my family and friends. To my wonderful editor Manda Waller for your years of expertise. To Debs Southwood and the team at Wigwam Studios for the brilliant book cover. I absolutely love it. A big thank you to Claire Hall for taking the time out of a hectic schedule to cast your proofreading eyes over my manuscript. A tremendous bear bug of a thank you to my wonderful partner Graeme who continues to be happy flying under the radar. And finally, where would I be without you, the reader? Thank you for making a gap in your life and jumping into the stories I've created. Here's to many more.

If you enjoyed Agnes Karapetsa is All at Sea, please consider leaving a review on Amazon and Goodreads. It really helps us self-published authors. And it's always lovely to hear your thoughts, so do get in touch on either TikTok, Facebook, Instagram or Twitter. All links are on www.jackiewatsonwrites.com, where you can sign up for my newsletter and find out what I'm up to.

Milton Keynes UK
Ingram Content Group UK Ltd.
UKHW041301141124
451200UK00005B/68

9 781739 340438